Cursed Bunny

Praise for the book

'While the stories in *Cursed Bunny* by Bora Chung blend elements of horror, fantasy and the surreal, each is viscerally rooted in the real fears and pressures of everyday life.'
– International Booker Prize judges

'Cool, brilliantly demented K-horror—just the way I like it!'
– Ed Park, author of *Personal Days*

'Whether borrowing from fable, folktale, speculative fiction, science fiction, or horror, Chung's stories corkscrew toward devastating conclusions—bleak, yes, but also wise and honest about the nightmares of contemporary life. Don't read this book while eating—but don't skip these unflinching, intelligent stories, either.'
– *Kirkus Reviews*

'[Chung's] glorious anglophone debut, enabled by award-winning Anton Hur, is poised to shock and delight. Bizarrely enigmatic, Chung's collection proves irresistible.'
– Terry Hong, *Booklist*

'Bora Chung's fascinating and unique short story collection, *Cursed Bunny*, displays the most disturbing truths about the nature of mankind through a fantastical yet realistic narrative.'
– *Asia Media International*

'The 10 stories are beyond imagination: breathtaking, wild, crazy, the most original fiction I have ever encountered.'
– Louisa Ermelino, *Publishers Weekly*

'If you were the kind of child who was enthralled by *Scary Stories to Read in the Dark,* Bora Chung writes for you. Like the work of Carmen Maria Machado and Aoko Matsuda, Chung's stories are so wonderfully, blisteringly strange and powerful that it's almost impossible to put *Cursed Bunny* down. In short, this collection may, in fact, be a cursed object in the best possible way.'
– Kelly Link, bestselling author of *Get in Trouble*

'Bora Chung's *Cursed Bunny* mines those places where what we fear is true and what is true meet and separate and re-meet. The resulting stories are indelible. Haunting, funny, gross, terrifying—and yet when we reach the end, we just want more.'
– Alexander Chee, author of *How to Write an Autobiographical Novel*

'Nothing concentrates the mind like Chung's terrors, which will shrivel you to a bouillon cube of your most primal instincts.'
– Rhoda Feng, *Vulture*

'Like a family in a home, fantastic stories gather together in this book. The stories not only take their revenge, but also love you, and comfort you. You'll end up completely endeared to this fascinating collection!'
– Kyung-sook Shin, *New York Times* bestselling author of *Please Look After Mom* and *Violets*

'A collection of exquisitely crafted, spooky and unnerving tales that haunted me long after reading. Each story is a macabre gem, shot through with visceral horror, wry humor, and subtly profound insights on human nature. These stories convey how the traumas and transgressions of the past, individual and collective, erupt into the present, distorting and eroding our perception of reality. Bora Chung is an amazingly inventive and daring writer. I will revisit these stories whenever I need a reminder of how fresh and vital prose can be.'
– Kate Folk, author of *Out There*

'What made this book truly transcendental was the sense of absolute dread that many of its stories summoned. Chung's work fits neatly beside that of Brian Evenson and Kelly Link—cerebral fiction that might give you nightmares.'
– Tobias Carroll, *Words Without Borders*

'Disturbing, chilling, wrenching, and absolute genius. I wanted Chung to write a story about a reader getting a deep look inside her fantastic swirling mind. I had to take breaks and gulps of air before plunging back into each story. Magnetic, eerie, immensely important.'
– Frances Cha, author of *If I Had Your Face*

'Fables of frightening moral clarity told in calm, bell-like prose, *Cursed Bunny* aims to unsettle. It's as assured and brilliant as a nightmare. With an unflinching gaze and a sly humor, Chung has built a world both unfamiliar and eerily familiar, whose truths echo into our own. The indelible work of a master.'
– Shruti Swamy, author of *The Archer* and *A House Is a Body*

Cursed Bunny

BORA CHUNG

Translated by Anton Hur

This translation first published in 2021 by Honford Star Ltd

First published in India in 2023 by Hachette India
(Registered name: Hachette Book Publishing India Pvt. Ltd)
An Hachette UK company
www.hachetteindia.com

4

ISBN 978-93-93701-61-9

For sale in the Indian Subcontinent only.

Hachette Book Publishing India Pvt. Ltd
4th & 5th Floors, Corporate Centre,
Plot No. 94, Sector 44, Gurugram 122003, India

Printed and bound in India
by Manipal Technologies Limited

Contents

The Head

She was about to flush the toilet.

"Mother?"

She looked back. There was a head popping out of the toilet, calling for her.

"Mother?"

The woman looked at it for a moment. Then, she flushed the toilet. The head disappeared in a rush of water.

She left the bathroom.

A few days later, she met the head again in the bathroom.

"Mother!"

The woman reached to flush the toilet again. The head sputtered, "N-no, just a minute ..."

The woman stayed her hand and looked down at the head in the toilet.

It was probably more accurate to refer to it as "a thing that vaguely looked like a head" than an actual head. It was about two-thirds the size of an adult's head and resembled a lump of carelessly slapped-together yellow and grey clay, with a few scattered clumps of wet hair. No ears, no eyebrows. Two slits for eyes so narrow that she couldn't tell if its eyes were open or closed. The crushed mound of flesh that was meant to be its nose. The mouth was also a lipless slit. This slit was awkwardly opening and closing as it talked to her, its strained speech mixed with the gurgling of a person drowning, making it difficult to understand.

"What in bloody hell are you?" the woman demanded.

"I call myself the head," the head replied.

"You would, obviously," the woman said, "but why are you in my toilet? And why are you calling me 'Mother'?"

The head strained as it formed unpracticed speech with its lipless mouth. "My body was created with the things you dumped down the toilet, like your fallen-out hair and feces and toilet paper you used to wipe your behind."

The woman became furious. "I never gave the likes of you any permission to live in my toilet. I never even created you in the first place, so stop calling me 'mommy.' Leave before I call the exterminators."

"I only want so little," the head hastily added, "I'm only asking that you keep dumping your body waste in the toilet so I can finish creating the rest of my body. Then I'll go far away from here and live by my own means. So please, just keep using the toilet like you always have."

"This is *my* toilet," the woman said coldly, "so of course I'm going to use it like I always have. But I can't bear to think of a creature like you living in it. Finishing your body is none of my concern. I don't care what you do, and I'd appreciate it if you stopped appearing."

The head disappeared into the toilet.

But the head kept reappearing.

After a flush, it would peer over the toilet seat and stare at the woman as she washed her hands. Whenever the woman felt like she was being watched, her eyes would dart to the toilet and lock gazes with its hard-to-tell-if-they-were-open eye slits. The mashed-up face seemed to be trying to create an expression, but it was impossible to tell what of. The head quickly disappeared down the toilet whenever she approached. The woman would then slam down the lid, flush, glare at the toilet for a while, and leave.

One day, the woman had used the toilet like always, flushed the bowl, and was washing her hands. The head appeared in the toilet behind her, as it normally did. The woman stared at it for a while through the mirror. The head stared back. The mashed-up face underneath the irregular clumps of hair would've normally been yellow and gray, but now it was oddly red.

The woman remembered she was having her period.

"Your color looks different," she said to the head. "Does it have anything to do with the state of my own body?"

The head replied, "Mother, the state of your body has a direct effect on my appearance. This is because my entire existence depends on you."

The woman took off her underwear and sanitary pad. She stuck the pad smeared with her menstrual blood on the head's face and shoved it down the toilet. She flushed.

The head and the pad swirled around the bowl and vanished into the dark hole. She washed her hands. Then, she vomited into the sink. She vomited for a long time, then rinsed the sink and left the bathroom.

The toilet got clogged. The plumber presented the sanitary pad to her as if it were a trophy and delivered a long lecture about not throwing such things into the toilet.

She began to keep her toilet lid closed. Whenever she was doing her business, she developed the habit of frequently looking into the bowl. The woman developed constipation.

One day, just as she was about to close the toilet lid, she caught a glimpse of the head peering out of the hole. She slammed down the lid. She flushed several times. Just as she was about to leave the bathroom, she carefully cracked open the lid. Her eyes met those of the head. It was staring at her from the water. Its hair floated around its face. She shut the lid again. She tried to flush but the water wouldn't go down.

The woman told her family about it.

"It's not like it's laying eggs or anything. Why don't you just leave it alone?"

And that was all her family said of the matter.

The woman avoided going to the bathroom at home.

One day, she saw it at her workplace bathroom. She had flushed the toilet and was washing her hands when she caught sight of, through the mirror, the head peeping out from the toilet in her stall. She quit her job the next day.

Her constipation worsened. Her bladder became inflamed. The doctor told her she needed to make regular visits to the bathroom. But the thought of something lurking below where she did her business, waiting to eat her defecations, made going to any bathroom unbearable.

The inflammation and constipation never really went away.

Now that she had quit her job, her family suggested she might as well find a husband. She went on a date set up by a matchmaker recommended by her mother. The man was an ordinary office worker at a trading company. He said his dream was to marry a nice woman, have children, and live happily ever after. He seemed unassuming and dependable, albeit unimaginative. Sitting before this strange man, she couldn't help being nervous about the bathroom situation. The man misconstrued her distracted fidgeting. He said, "My ideal woman is shy and demure. It's hard to find a girl like you who's shy in front of a man these days."

The man was so enamored and enthusiastic about the match that they were engaged three months later and wedded in another three.

Now she was worried about the honeymoon. Thankfully, the head didn't appear on the trip. The first thing she checked after moving into her new home with her husband was the toilet. There was nothing inside. Life in her new home brought some relief to her bladder inflammation and constipation. Days had no highs or lows, weren't particularly good or bad, and she thought herself more or less content. In the whirlwind of adjusting to her new life, she found herself thinking less and less about the head. Soon, she had a child and forgot about the head completely.

It was shortly after the birth of her child when the head reappeared in her life. She had been bathing the little one in a baby basin.

"Mother."

She almost drowned her child by accident.

The head's head had now grown to about the size of an average adult's. The yellow and gray mashed-up clay lump form was the same, but its eyes were a little bigger so she could now make out its blinking, and something that resembled lips was attached to its mouth. There were mounds of flesh for ears that looked like they'd been carelessly stuck on either side of its face, and beneath its barely discernible chin was a new band of flesh that seemed to be the beginnings of a neck.

"Mother, is that child your daughter?"

The woman sputtered, "How is it that you have reappeared before me? Who told you where we were?"

The head replied, "Your defecations are a part of me, so I will always know where you are."

The head's words displeased the woman. She hissed, "I told you to go away. How dare you reappear calling me 'Mother'! It's none of your concern whose child this is! But fine, this is my child. She is the only one in this world who may call me 'Mother.' Now, be gone. I said, be gone!" The child started to wail.

The head said, "I may have been birthed a different way from that child, but I, too, am your creation, Mother."

"Did I not say that I never created the likes of you? I told you to be gone. If you refuse, I shall do whatever it takes to find and destroy you!"

She slammed down the toilet lid and flushed. Then, she consoled her crying child and wiped off the remaining soap suds.

Once the head came back into her life, it kept reappearing like a bad rash. She could feel it staring at her from behind after she had flushed and was washing her hands. She could see something yellow and gray in the corner of her eye, but when she quickly turned to look, it was gone, leaving only a few tell-tale strands of hair floating in the toilet bowl.

Her constipation and bladder inflammation returned. More than anything else, she was worried for the child. Was the head jealous of her daughter? Would it bully the child? Just the thought of the child glimpsing the head was unbearable. She became nervous whenever the little one wanted to go to the bathroom.

She clenched her fists. She was going to destroy the head.

The woman went to the bathroom, did her business, and flushed. She waited for the head to appear as she washed her hands. When a yellow and gray thing slowly rose from the toilet bowl, the woman said in a low voice, "I have something to say to you."

She finished washing her hands and crouched down before the toilet so she was eye-to-eye with the head.

"You are …"

She hesitated. The head waited.

She grabbed the head, easily plucked it from the toilet, and wrapped it in a plastic bag. She threw the bag away in a trash can outside. Then, with a light heart, she went back to living her life.

The reprieve didn't last long. She was in the bathroom with the child when it happened. The child was now old enough to get on the toilet by herself. Her daughter could pretty much handle the whole process if the woman reminded her of every step, from lowering her underwear, sitting on the toilet and doing her business, wiping her behind, putting on her clothes again, flushing, and washing her hands. However, her daughter wasn't tall enough to reach the sink yet, so the woman had to hoist her up to the sink to soap her hands. One day, as the woman was doing so, a familiar yellow and gray thing appeared.

"Mother."

The woman turned around and saw the head. Then, she finished rinsing off the suds from the child's hands, dried them on a towel, and sent her daughter out the bathroom.

"Mother."

"What's the meaning of this? How are you back?"

The mouth of the head almost imperceptibly twisted into a sneer. "I begged the janitor who found me to flush me down the toilet."

The woman said nothing as she flushed the toilet. The head swirled in the rushing of the water as it disappeared down the dark hole.

Outside the bathroom, the child was full of questions. She told her child, "That was what we call a 'head.' If you see it again, just flush."

The head had the gall to appear before her and the child and call her "Mother." She decided she had to get rid of it once and for all.

Plucking the head from the toilet again was easy. But just as she was about to wrap it in a plastic bag and throw it out with the garbage, she hesitated. The head could talk. If she threw it out like this, it could ask someone to flush it down the toilet like last time. She had to ensure that it couldn't talk.

The woman shoved the head into a small container, which she put in a sunny spot on the veranda. She figured that without water or more defecation, the head would eventually mummify. She couldn't think of any other way, nor did she care to expend further effort on the issue.

She cautioned her husband and child to not disturb the container. Her husband had no occasion to go out on the veranda, but her child was curious. Her daughter squirmed with the desire to poke and stare and talk to it. The woman gave the child a harsh scolding and hid the container with the head.

Her husband received some vacation time, and they went traveling for a few days. When they returned, the woman went to the bathroom. She was washing her hands when something appeared behind her. She turned around. She slammed down the lid of the toilet seat and flushed.

The woman scolded the child. "You did this, didn't you! I told you over and over again not to touch it!"

The child began to cry. Her husband stepped in. "Oh, that thing in the container? It asked me to put it in the toilet, so I did. Why, did I do something wrong?"

She sighed and told him the whole story.

Her husband remained nonchalant. "Eh, that's nothing. Just leave it alone. It's not like it crawls out of there at night and lays eggs around the house."

The woman dreamed she was in a white, tiled room. Suddenly, the head popped out from behind her. The woman turned around in surprise. Then, the head popped out from another direction. It began popping out from everywhere.

Next to her, her delighted daughter kept pointing at it. "Head! Head!"

The woman begged her husband for help. He was sitting on her other side reading a newspaper. "Eh, that's nothing. Just leave it alone."

His words bounced against the tiles and chorused off the walls. *Leave it alone. That's nothing. Leave it alone. That's nothing.*

The lever for the flush was near the ceiling. She reached it with some difficulty and just managed to pull it. Water swirled around her husband, her child, and the head. The woman got sucked into a dark hole along with her still delighted child and her still nonchalantly newspaper-reading husband. She grabbed her child and tried with all her might to escape the whirlpool. A familiar voice spoke in her ear.

"Mother?"

She looked down at her child. Upon her daughter's little body and delicate neck sat the head.

The shock woke her. She stumbled into the bathroom. She sat in front of the toilet and stared into the pure, flawless white of the bowl, the clear water pooled inside, and the dark hole submerged within. Imagining the thing inside and where that hole led to.

But ever since she had tried to mummify it, the head no longer appeared. And as time went on, she no longer had nightmares about it. The woman quietly went about her life—cooking for her husband and child, washing the dishes, doing the laundry, cleaning the house, shopping, and generally immersing herself in years comprised of unremarkable, peaceful days. Her husband moved up in his company, no faster or slower than others. The man wasn't especially gentle or warm, but he did bring home a cake on her or their child's birthday and placed candles on it. Her child, like everyone else, went to elementary school, then to middle school, and became a high school student. The child's grades weren't particularly good or bad. She was cute, but no beauty queen. She was a typical high school student who had trouble getting up in the morning, liked celebrities, and fretted over her pimples in the mirror.

"Come get breakfast or you'll be late."

"Mom, did you see my uniform necktie?"

"I hung it on the doorknob of your bedroom. Slow down, you'll get an upset stomach."

"OK. Oh, by the way, I saw a person's head in the toilet yesterday."

"Did you now. What happened?"

"I just flushed it down the toilet."

"Good. More stew?"

"I'm good. But about that head, I think I've seen it before. Is there a way to get rid of it? It's vile."

"Forget about it. Just flush it down again. Are you done?"

"Yup. See you later."

"You've packed your lunch?"

"I did. Bye, Mom."

"Have a good day."

The door closed.

Forget about it.

That's nothing.

The woman began clearing the table.

Her child entered college. Meanwhile, she started noticing wrinkles and sagging skin, and rough patches in places that had once been smooth. She gave her child some lipstick and it suited the girl well, only the child wasn't a girl anymore but a young lady. The woman rediscovered the contours of her younger face in the familiar-unfamiliar face of her daughter, feeling surprise, pride, love, and jealousy at the same time. When her child straight-permed her hair flat and dyed it purple, the woman stood before a mirror when no one was watching and fiddled with the curls of her "auntie perm," a tight cap of poodle-like hair that had to be dyed black.

The woman spent more and more time alone in the house. Her husband had been promoted to the executive level and lived under a mountain of work and her child was also busy with her own life, so the family rarely saw each other during the day. From time to time, her husband came home a little earlier than usual and the two of them spent a quiet evening together, but they had never had a fiery romance to begin with or had much in terms of memories to fall back on. They had spent too much of their marriage in a state of emotional detachment to really start making an effort to be affectionate now. They usually ate dinner in silence, watched some television in silence, and her husband would go to bed first in silence.

The woman would then watch TV on her own. On days her child or husband came home late, or even after her whole family had long fallen asleep, she would watch TV until the national anthem came on. Partly because she had nothing else to do, but more so because she thought if she concentrated hard enough on the screen, she might decrease an odd-feeling little space that had appeared in her heart. The space felt empty sometimes, full at others, and bitter or aching at still other times. This strange little space, if she ever let her guard down, could suddenly blow up in size and consume her. So she kept watching TV, trying to empty her heart and mind as she gazed upon the meaningless progression of scenes on the screen. But the well of thought taps a deep spring, and no matter how much she tried to bail them out, her thoughts kept overflowing the brim …

Then one night, she went to the bathroom.

She had been watching TV, like always, and was alone in the house, like always. She did her business, closed the lid, and flushed. While washing her hands, she glanced at herself in the mirror. Sagging eyelids, wrinkles, rough and dry skin. White hair peeking out from the roots of her dye job. She was fiddling with her hair, thinking she'd need another hair appointment soon, when she saw, through the mirror, the lid of the toilet seat move.

Clack.

A wet hand rose from inside the toilet and pushed the lid open. Another wet hand emerged. The two hands gripped the edge of the toilet.

She watched as the back of a person's head, thick with hair and slick with water, rose from the toilet bowl.

The delicate hands spread their long, thin fingers and pushed down against the rim, bringing up a narrow pair of fine-boned shoulders and slender arms. The rich black hair reached all the way down the smooth back, followed by the sensuous line of a svelte waist and white, voluptuous buttocks and firm thighs. A knee rose up and a foot perched on the edge of the toilet bowl. The leg was white and long and slim. The calves were precisely the right size, the muscles tensing a little as the foot was brought up, the ankle dainty. The other foot emerged, and its exquisite toes lightly touched down on the bathroom floor. The drenched, naked body shone in the yellow, dim light of the bathroom.

The woman kept staring into the mirror. The person who had emerged from the toilet slowly turned around. The woman saw the face of her youth reflected next to her own sagging face. Her young self, smiling at her old self.

The old self slowly turned around to face the young self.

The head that was no longer a head stood still. The old self stared back at the face of her youth, a face that continued to smile at her.

"Mother?" The tone of voice was a little high-pitched but there was no more of the old gurgling sound, no more of that irritating voice of a person drowning. "Do you recognize me?"

"Well …" Her own voice creaked like a rusty hinge.

"How have you been, Mother?"

The woman said nothing.

"I have finished my body. And just as I promised, I shall leave and live by my own means. I'm here to say goodbye and ask a final request."

One word pricked her attention: "Request."

"Don't worry." The head smiled as if to reassure her. "I can't very well go out in the world naked now, can I? It was hard enough finishing my body with just what you were giving me, so I had no means to create garments to cover myself. This is my first and last request. If you could just give me a change of clothing, I shall hide my shameful parts and be on my way."

The woman thought of the clothes hanging in her wardrobe and turned to leave the bathroom. The head stopped her.

"Don't go out of your way. Just the clothes you're wearing now will do fine."

The woman replied, "What are you talking about? You want me to take off my clothes for you this minute? On the freezing floor tiles? You should just take what I give you—why are you being so demanding?"

"Mother, please calm down." The head gazed at her with an expression of longing on her young face. "I've never received anything from you besides what you've thrown away. This is my first and last request. If you give me the clothes you're wearing now, I shall keep the heat and scent of you forever with me until the day I die, with gratitude."

The woman stared at her younger self. At her younger body. At this individual created not through a womb and placenta but through the colon and defecation. She stared at what had hidden in the dark hole in the white porcelain all that time, torturing her, and was now declaring independence. If this really was goodbye, and if they really were never to see each other again, what was a change of clothing to her?

As her young self toweled off, the old self stripped down. Her garments weren't anything fancy: a cardigan, a simple dress, a bra, panties, and socks. That was it. Naked, she watched her young self pick up each item and put them on. Panties. Bra. Dress. Cardigan. Her young self seemed to relish each item. Lastly, the socks were put on, the buttons on the cardigan done up. Her old self felt a chill against her naked body.

"All right, then. Now that you've put on my clothes, be off. I'm cold. I need to put something on."

She turned again to leave the bathroom.

Her young self swiftly came between her and the door.

"*Where do you think you're going*? Your place is not out here." She pointed to the toilet. "It's in *there*."

"What are you going on about?" cried the old self. "Did I not give you clothes when you asked for them? Did I not do everything you told me to? Why are you so ungrateful? Enough with this insanity, be off. Be off!"

A sneer transformed her young self's face. "That's right. You gave me everything I told you to, and all you have left is that old lump of a body. For too long, I've endured down there while you got to enjoy your life on the outside, all this time. Now it's your turn to go down the toilet. I shall take your place and enjoy everything you've enjoyed!"

The old self was furious. "You ingrate! What was there to *enjoy* out here? My life is the same as everyone else's, and did you not, with your torture, ruin what little happiness I had? I withstood all that disgust and hate and made you who you are today. If you have any gratitude for what I've done for you despite everything that you've put me through, then use your finished body to disappear from my life! Get out of my sight!"

The sneer faded from her young self's face. With flashing eyes, her young self spoke through clenched teeth, but in a clear, slow, and restrained tone. "Gratitude. What gratitude should I have for you? Did I ask you to give birth to me? Did you ever take care of me or even say a kind word to me, your indisputable offspring? You birthed me even when I didn't want it, and did you not try at every turn to destroy me out of hatred and disgust? What have you given me besides your feces and trash? I had to bear all sorts of humiliations and degradations to get what I needed from you to complete a human-like body. But now, it's complete. This is the day I've been waiting for in that dark hole all my life. Now that I have become you, I shall take your place and live a new life."

The young approached the old. Young, strong hands gripped old shoulders and neck. The young hands shoved the old's head into the toilet and quick as a flash, lifted her by the ankles. Lightly shoving the old body into the toilet, her young self closed the lid shut and flushed.

The Embodiment

몸하다: *"to body." To menstruate. To undergo menstruation.*

The bleeding refused to stop. It was twelve days into her cycle. Usually the flow began to lessen around the third day and ended on the fifth, but it was now almost two weeks without any sign of stopping. The flow seemed to taper off at night but would inevitably return by dawn.

A fortnight later, the blood still flowed; should she see a gynecologist? But the gynecologist's office was not a place a young unmarried woman could visit without feeling oddly guilty.

After the twentieth day, the dizziness began, and she became so tired that it was starting to affect her daily functioning. She gritted her teeth and went to see a doctor.

The gynecologist wordlessly slathered a transparent, slippery gel on her belly and passed a cold metal disc over it. He mumbled as he stared into a foggy black-and-white display, "I don't see anything strange ..."

She wiped off the gel as best she could—it kept getting

all over her hands and clothes no matter how vigorously she mopped—and went back to the consultation room. The doctor glanced at the chart before him and asked, "Have you been very stressed lately? Or had any big changes in your environment?"

"I'm writing my master's thesis ... But I don't think I'm *that* stressed about it ..."

The doctor gave her a look before scribbling something down.

"Stress causes hormonal imbalances that can lead to your situation. According to the ultrasound you're fine, so I'll prescribe you some birth control pills. Take them for three weeks, go off them for one, then take them for three weeks more, then rest for a week, and so on. You'll be back to normal in two to three months."

She began taking birth control pills.

She took them for three weeks and had a week off. Then three weeks more before quitting after those two months. But her period, which began two days after she had quit, refused to stop for over ten days. This meant going back on the pills, and like clockwork, the blood stopped. When she tried to get off the pills again three weeks later, the same thing happened. She ended up having to foot the unexpected expense of taking six months of birth control pills.

After six months, her period went back to normal, ceasing after five days. She cheered.

Another month later, she got out of bed one morning but had to sit back down when the world began to spin.

She dry-heaved all day. The dizziness was unbearable and

nothing she ate stayed down. She felt sluggish and had a touch of fever.

A full-body check-up was in order. At a big hospital, she got her X-rays taken and her blood and urine examined.

The doctor informed her of her results in an emotionless manner. "You're pregnant."

"Excuse me?"

"You should see an obstetrician."

She went down a few floors to see one of the hospital's obstetricians—a young woman in her thirties who wore an unbelievable amount of makeup. After a few more fairly unpleasant examinations, the obstetrician declared her diagnosis in an ice-cold voice. "You're six weeks pregnant."

"But I'm unmarried and have no boyfriend."

"You've never had any sexual experiences? Or taken any pills?"

"I did take some birth control pills for a while because my period wouldn't stop—"

"For how long?"

"Six months."

The doctor gave her a sharp look, narrowing her bright blue eyeshadowed, thickly penciled eyes.

"Were they prescribed?"

"The doctor told me to take them for a couple of months, and you don't really need a prescription for birth control pills ..." Her voice trailed off as she felt oddly ashamed.

"If the doctor told you to take them for just two to three months, you should've taken them for just two to three months!"

"Well, uh, my period just wouldn't stop ..."

The doctor sighed her irritation out her vividly painted red lips. "If your body happens to be abnormal, a side effect from taking birth control pills for a long time can be pregnancy."

"Really? But ... aren't birth control pills made to prevent pregnancy?" Her objection came out meek.

The doctor's black-and-blue gaze immediately turned sharp again. "You're the one who overdid it with the pills—it's your own fault. Medicine isn't candy you can gorge on whenever you feel like it."

"What ... what do I do now?"

The doctor flipped through the chart. "Does the child have a father?"

"Excuse me?"

"Does the child have someone who can be their father?"

"No ..."

The doctor looked up and again gave her a scary look through her thick makeup. "Then you better hurry up and find a man who's willing to be the father."

"The child's father? Why?"

The doctor shot back, "You're carrying a child—of course the child needs a father!"

"But, uh, what happens if there's no father?"

"You're in a situation where you've become pregnant under abnormal circumstances, which means that if you don't find a male partner, the cells of the fetus will not properly propagate or grow. You know how in grocery stores there are free-range fertilized eggs and non-fertilized eggs? It's the same thing here. If the fetus does not properly grow, then your pregnancy will not proceed normally, and this will ultimately be bad for the mother. Do you understand what I'm saying?" Clearly, the doctor was annoyed with her.

"W-what do you mean bad?"

"That depends. You're only six weeks along right now, so I can't really tell you what's going to happen." The doctor sighed. Then, she glared at her again and threatened, "You better find a father for that child, fast. If you don't, things will really get bad for you."

Her family concluded that she should take a leave of absence from school and get set up by a matchmaker before she began to show. She wrote "sickness" on the request form as her reason for taking leave. Her short-tempered thesis advisor threw a fit over her taking a break just when her thesis was finally shaping up. She regretted the interruption in her work as well, but there was nothing to be done. The people in her department commiserated with her as if she had contracted a fatal disease.

She didn't have much to do once she had left school. Her family became busy instead, coming together for the great "Find the Child a Father" project. It wasn't long before her mother and the matchmaker had set up her first matchmaking seon date at a café.

An awkward silence descended between her and the man as soon as the matchmaker and her mother left the table. This was her first time on a seon date, and she didn't know what to say to this complete stranger or where to look or what to do with her hands. Her morning sickness, which had seemed to ebb, had come back that morning with a vengeance, and the strong air-conditioning breeze of the fancy hotel café, coupled with the smell of the black coffee, was making her shiver and her insides flip-flop.

The man, somewhat apologetically, began to speak. "So … you're a graduate student?"

"Yes …" Her lips were blue from the cold and she could barely manage to answer him through her shivering.

"What are you specializing in?"

"Slavic literature—"

"How very unusual! I'm sure there can't be many people studying Norwegian literature in Korea?"

"Uh, that's not quite—"

She suddenly couldn't stand the smell of the coffee. Casting her dignity to the winds, she bolted from her seat and sprinted to the ladies' room. For a long time, she wrung out nothing from her stomach other than a little coffee, air, and bile. She prayed the man had left as she washed her mouth and hands.

But he was waiting for her in front of the ladies' room with worry written all over his face. He quickly supported her arm as she came stumbling out the door. "Are you all right?"

"Yes … I'm so sorry."

She was bright red and didn't know what to do with herself. The man helped her back to their table. As she leaned on him during the short distance of their slow walk back, she noticed how his shoulders were wide enough to wrap around hers in an embrace. Her hands and shoulders, freezing from the air-conditioning, registered that the man's arm was strong and hard, but at the same time warm and appealing. The room was still spinning, her legs threatened to give way, and she was so ashamed that she wanted to make a run for it, but as she became conscious of these facts about his body, her red face grew even more crimson.

"Are you very unwell? Shall we go?"

"I'm sorry, may I sit down for a bit?"

"Oh, of course."

She collapsed into the chair and couldn't think of anything to say to him. The man, not knowing what to do, kept sipping his coffee.

"Are you sick today? I hope you didn't force yourself to come out ..."

"No, it's just morning sickness ... I'm pregnant, you see."

"Oh, really? Congratulations."

"Thank you."

"Then it must be the smell of the coffee that made you uncomfortable. Shall we get rid of it?" He immediately called over a waiter.

"Thank you so much." She was still mortified, but it was a relief not to have to smell the coffee anymore.

"But you mustn't be too far along?"

"Yes, it's only been two months."

"So you don't know if it's a boy or a girl? I'm sorry, I'm being nosy."

"Oh no, that's fine. I don't know yet. I didn't ask, on purpose."

"I guess it's more fun to wait and have the anticipation."

The man was polite and kind, an unexpectedly nice conversation partner. She felt attracted to him. They talked for a while about pregnancy and babies until she suddenly asked him, "So, um, would you be my child's father?"

"The child's father?"

"Yes, to be honest, that's why I'm on this seon date ..." She gave a quick summary and confession as to how she became pregnant through the birth control pills and the doctor's warning.

The man listened with a sincere expression. After she finished, he seemed lost in thought for a moment. "Well ... I think I'd have to think about it a bit more. I didn't know this was your situation when I agreed to come ... I know it's a seon date but becoming a father is not an easy decision. I hope you understand."

"Of course, that's fine."

"I can't give you an answer right now, but maybe if we saw each other a bit more and got to know each other better, I'd be able to decide then. Would that be all right?"

"Very much so."

The man insisted on driving her home despite her repeated refusals.

"I'm actually a driver by trade. You can trust me," He said this with a smile.

As she watched him drive off into the night after dropping her off by her house, she thought of how they had talked all afternoon and the only thing she really knew about him was the fact that he was a driver.

She went on a string of seon dates with other men after that, but nothing really took. There were many times where she would run to the ladies' room and come back to find the man had disappeared. Some of the men became tense and took out their cigarettes at the mention of her being pregnant and others made sure she was aware of their distaste for her situation. She kept thinking that the first man had been the best, but his irregular work hours made it difficult to keep in constant contact with him.

Slowly but surely, her stomach grew. The pregnancy became obvious at five months. Her morning sickness seemed to get worse for a time but eventually began to abate. Her breasts grew bigger and her weight climbed to the point where her back and feet hurt. She became out of breath easily and her ankles frequently swelled up. She often felt a knot in her chest, sweated like a fiend, and was constantly in and out of the bathroom. The hospital assured her that these were all normal signs of pregnancy. But at six months, there was no longer any fetal movement. She only felt a slight twisting or trembling inside of her, but these weren't the sensations of a baby kicking inside her womb.

The thickly made-up obstetrician sneered at her worries. "You still haven't found a father for the child? This is all because of that."

"Well, I mean, it's not so easy—"

"Nothing in life is easy! Did you really think pregnancy would be easy? What are you trying to do about it? Do you have any idea how little time you have left?"

"I'm looking, but—"

"If this is your attitude now, what kind of a mother do you think you're going to be? Think about it. There's a new life growing in your belly right this minute. A human being is being created. You have to take responsibility for an entire human being! But if you're this nonchalant at the fetus' development stage, what are you going to do once you give birth?"

"But that's—"

"You seem to be complacent because you can't actually see the baby right now, but keep this up and you'll *really* see what you're doing to the baby. If you want a normal child, you'll do whatever it takes to find a father."

"But I really am trying to find the baby a good father, for the sake of the *child*—"

"You're running out of time!"

The top of the obstetrician's head seemed about to pop off far above her layers of blue eyeshadow and black eyeliner—her narrowed stare so sharp that it threatened to cut anyone who met it.

Defeated, she quickly left the hospital.

It wasn't easy going about seeing people with her protruding belly. When the man on her thirty-seventh seon date took one look at her stomach and fled the café without a word, she declared that she would no longer go on anymore seon dates. She made a big show of proclaiming that she had conceived on her own and therefore would raise the baby on her own. But she couldn't do anything about the persistent worry and fear that tormented her, that she was somehow irreparably harming the child by having this baby without a father.

Her daily routine devolved into keeping herself comfortable in bed and listening to music and watching videos that were said to be good for expecting mothers. She ate foods high in iron because her morning sickness had been replaced by anemia. Her sense of taste didn't change however, nor did she suddenly crave foods she normally disliked. Her days were slow and peaceful, and all of her relatives who would usually never give her a second thought were suddenly very interested in her well-being and treated her like a fragile heirloom, always making sure to ask if there was anything she might want. Aside from the times she had to go to the obstetrician for examinations, her life had settled down and she felt content.

One day, as she read fairy tales for expecting mothers while listening to music for expecting mothers, her phone buzzed. It was a text message.

Call me immediately.

She had never seen the number before. Figuring it was a wrong number, she deleted the message.

Ten minutes later, her phone buzzed again. It was the same message. She deleted it.

Fifteen minutes later, her phone buzzed yet again. The same message. This time, there were exclamation marks.

Call me!! Immediately!!

Someone with an emergency must have the wrong number. She pressed dial.

"Hello?" answered an unfamiliar male voice.

"Hello? Did you send me a text just now?"

"Are you Kim Young-lan?"

This surprised her. "Yes, I'm Kim Young-lan. Who are you?"

She heard a rustling sound.

"Itseu my lady, oh, itseu my lobeu! Oh, datseu, I mean, dat she, she new she wuh! She seu-peak-seu yet she seseu no, I mean, nuh-ssing, wut obeu det? Huh eye diseu, dee, deesu-co-ssiseu, ah-ee will en-suh it, ah-im too boldeu, uh, teu, tiseu nat to me she seu-peakseu—"

(It is my lady, O, it is my love! / O, that she knew she were! / She speaks yet she says nothing: what of that? / Her eye discourses; I will answer it, / I am too bold, 'tis not to me she speaks—)

"Um ... hello?"

The man continued, his voice slightly louder, *"Too obeu duh peh, peh-uh-resteu staseu in oll duh heh-beun, heh-bing sum bee-jeu-nee-seu, do, uh, en, entreeteu huh ah-iseu, to, to teu-in-kle—"*

(Two of the fairest stars in all the heaven, / Having some business, do entreat her eyes / To twinkle ...)

"Hold on!" she shouted. The man stopped his recitation. "What on Earth are you doing?"

"It's from Shakespeare's *Romeo and Juliet*. Second act, second scene, in the Capulets' garden."

"Excuse me?"

"It's how I feel. I knew the moment I saw your picture in the paper. You are the woman of my destiny. *Oh, yu, ah, my, ro-seu, my buhning ha-teu—"*

"In the paper? What paper?"

"I could really sense your womanliness from the headline: 'Looking for a Man to Be My Child's Father.' Such a cut above the usual pandering for a husband! Such femininity, such literary sensitivity. My darling Young-lan, we are meant to be.

Through our passion for literature, *too-geh-duh dee-peu luh-beu endeu un-duh-seu-ten-ding—*"

"Look, you have the wrong idea—"

"I may be so poor that I committed the faux pas of asking you to call me instead of calling you first, but I will pay you back for the phone call someday. Capitalism is nothing before the forces of love and passion! *Oh, my lay-ee-dee, my leh-deu roseu—*"

"I'm not an English major!"

She slammed down the phone and looked for a newspaper. On the very last page was her photograph accompanied by large letters: LOOKING FOR A MAN TO BE MY CHILD'S FATHER. Her name and age were next to the photo along with "Graduate student, literature" as her occupation. Her phone number, clearly printed, underneath that.

At the dinner table, she brandished the newspaper and berated her family. They glanced at each other and said it had been a last-ditch effort to get her child a father.

"We thought it might be easier if we were just honest about it up front ..."

She was annoyed, but thinking back on the obstetrician's warning, she couldn't help but agree just a little. She suffered through many phone calls after that. But she did have a glimmer of hope before picking up every call.

When she refused to answer Romeo's pleading texts, he began calling her. Every day, it was a new scene from a play of some male character wooing a woman, topped off with his begging her to meet him. There were prank calls from children, as well as serious calls from women offering to introduce her to their brothers, fathers, sons, even husbands. There were threats, too.

"Hello?"

"Is this Ms. Kim Young-lan?"

"Yes?"

"Remember me, bitch?"

"What?"

"We fucked. Don't you remember? Your baby is my baby."

"Uh, I think you've dialed the wrong—"

"Enough with this bullshit. Let's talk. Bring ten million won to the MM Hotel coffee shop at noon tomorrow. Then I'll keep it a secret."

"Excuse me, what was the number you wanted to call?"

"Are you stupid or something? Is tomorrow too soon? All right, I'll cut you a break. You have until this weekend to come to the MM Hotel coffee shop with the money. Or else I'm going to go around your neighborhood saying that we fucked and that your baby is mine. Understand? Everyone is going to know what a slut you are."

"Actually, that's exactly what I need, a man to be the father—"

"Your future is at stake so think about it. Ten million won until this weekend. Got it?"

He hung up.

She suffered through many more pointless calls. Then one day, she finally received a somewhat promising one.

"Hello?"

"Hello, I'm calling in answer of an ad. Are you Kim Younglan?" The man's voice was young and polite.

"This is she."

"You said you were looking for a father for the child, right? Do you have any specific requirements? Age, or that kind of thing ..."

She hadn't thought that far ahead. She answered vaguely, "Well, I don't know about any requirements, I guess as long as it's someone who can be a good father—"

"Oh, really?" The man seemed to think for a while. "Then how does one apply to be the child's father?"

She grinned, thinking he was an interesting person. "You don't need to put in an application. Could you tell me about yourself?"

"Oh, how rude of me." He went on to say he was thirty-three years old, a graduate of a top school, and currently working at a conglomerate. Having never worked in a corporate setting, she wasn't sure what his job title really meant, but she had a feeling that he was in a very high position for someone so young. Really, a flawless candidate. Even if he were lying, and it was true she was a little suspicious, she found herself liking the overall impression he gave off as a person. More than anything else, she liked that he had asked her what she was looking for in a father. After a long conversation, they made a date to meet at the MM Hotel coffee shop on the weekend and hung up.

On the day of the date, she chose the most business-like maternity dress she had, carefully applied her makeup, and went to the café with her heart pounding and her arms hugging her belly.

At the entrance, as she stood for a moment looking around,

wondering who might be her date, a young man approached her.

"Are you Kim Young-lan?"

"I am."

The man whose voice she recognized from the phone was exceptionally handsome. She followed him to a table. There was an old man sitting there, and two men wearing sunglasses standing at attention behind him.

The young man introduced the old one. "This is my father-in-law."

"Excuse me?"

"I'll leave you two alone, then."

"Uh, could you wait a minute ..."

The young man left the café.

The old man spoke. "Sit down."

One of the sunglassed men behind him pulled out a chair. Not knowing what else to do, she sat down.

"I'll get straight to the point. I'm Suh Woochang, head of the Woochang Group." This startled her. "The man that just left, he's my son-in-law. I'm the last in eight generations of only sons. I had no children until I was fifty, and only had one daughter. We poured all our care into her, but she ended up with that useless piece of garbage you just saw. I was going to overlook it and pass on the company if they had a son, but it's already been six years with no child. I ended up with a dickless piece of shit for a son-in-law and for that, I'm about to lose everything I worked my whole life for."

He was getting worked up by his own story. She was finding the situation more and more confusing.

"So anyways, young lady." He suddenly shifted closer to her and grabbed her hand. "That child in your belly, give it to me. The field is already tilled and all you need is the seed, right? I'll give you my seed. Or why not come into my house as a concubine? You just have to continue our line, give me a nice, fat son, and I'll make sure you and the child will live a happy life."

"Uh, excuse me, grandfather, but—"

"My idiot son-in-law tells me you said age wasn't an issue. I'm eighty-two, but as hot-blooded as any young man. I'll put your name down on the family registry and everything, what do you say?"

"Grandfather, that's not—" As she desperately sought a way out of this mess, trying to extract her hand from his, her phone rang. Relieved, she finally managed to snatch her hand back and answer the phone.

"Hello?"

But there was no answer and the line went dead. The old man grabbed her hand again.

"What do you say, young lady? Give me a son and you'll live the rest of your life in luxury as a chaebol wife. It's a once-in-a-lifetime opportunity."

"Kim Young-lan?"

She looked up. A cruel-faced middle-aged man stood before her.

"You know who I am, right? Did you bring the ten million won?"

"Who the hell are you?" the old man asked, frowning at this interloper.

"Me?" The other man took out a cigarette from his shirt pocket, lit it, and blew a plume of smoke into the old man's face. The sunglassed men behind the old man took a step forward, but the old man held up a hand to halt them. The men took a step back.

The middle-aged man puffed leisurely on his cigarette. "I'm this woman's lover. The baby in her belly is mine."

"What?"

"Are you her father? Or some old pervert trying to buy her for sex? Jesus, did I hit the jackpot this time." He smiled at the old man, brought his face down within an inch of the old man's, and said in a low, threatening voice, "I don't know if she's your precious daughter or your trophy wife, but if you don't want everyone to think she's having my baby, you better hand over fifty million won, fast."

"What the hell is this bastard saying!" The old man shouted so loudly that the sunglassed men stepped up to them again.

The middle-aged man didn't back down. "Bastard? Who are you calling bastard? If you know what's good for you, hand over the money while I'm feeling generous. Then I'll be on my way."

The old man looked at her and the middle-aged man and went, "Huh!" and stood up, whacking his cane on the floor. The sunglassed men hurried to support him.

"Where the fuck do you think you're going?" The middle-aged man grabbed the old man by the collar. "Do you think this is some—oof!"

One of the sunglassed men had swiftly punched the middle-aged man in the stomach. He rolled about on the floor as the goons turned to leave with the old man.

"You fucking bastards, you hit me!" He leaped at the three departing men, and the four of them ended up on the floor in a tangled heap of bodies. One of the sunglassed men quickly began to help the old man up while the other mercilessly beat up the middle-aged man. The café customers screamed. A hotel worker frantically called someone on the phone.

Carefully avoiding the fighting, she slipped out on her own.

Her heart felt many times heavier than her belly as she walked to the bus stop. She felt stupid, yet also couldn't help but laugh at the ridiculousness of the situation just now.

The bus arrived. She tried not to fall flat on her face as she made her way up the steps. The bus driver watched with annoyance and started driving before she had made it completely up. She almost fell but grabbed the bus card scanner just in time.

Although the bus wasn't that crowded, there were no empty seats. She wanted to go to the back as she had a long way to go, but it was hard to keep her balance in the shaky bus; she grabbed a pole near the driver's seat and hung on for dear life.

"Young lady, sit here," said the middle-aged woman sitting near her.

"Oh, I'm all right, thank you."

"It doesn't look like you're all right at all!" The woman smiled warmly as she pretended to admonish her. "Your stomach is as big as Namsan Mountain, how could it be all right to stay standing on a shaking bus? You're making me all nervous! Sit down this minute."

"Thank you so much." She gave an embarrassed smile as she gingerly sat down with the help of the older woman.

Just as she settled down, the middle-aged woman looked closely at her face and blurted out, "Hey, aren't you the girl from the newspaper?"

"Excuse me?" But she knew what was coming and her heart was sinking to her stomach.

"You know, the one who's looking for a father for her child?"

"Uh ..." She was still in shock from what had happened in the café, and the very mention of the ad made her want to cry. She bitterly regretted not having cancelled the ad sooner.

"The real father must've run away after you got pregnant, am I right?" The older woman was already weaving her own story about her. "You poor thing. How could he leave such a young and pretty girl?"

The middle-aged woman patted her back like she was her real mother. It was infuriating and she was indignant, but at the same time, the woman's warm hand did feel like it was gently patting away the hurt.

"I mean, that's life," the older woman went on to say. "And life goes on. Think of the child in your belly. Live only for the child. It's not easy raising a kid alone these days, but you've got to be strong and keep living your life! Children grow up so fast. Mark my words, today will seem like a distant memory soon enough ..."

The woman's voice trailed off as she gazed into the distance.

Screech. The bus came to a stop. The older woman quickly came to her senses. "Oh, my goodness, where am I?" She quickly pressed the stop buzzer and frantically looked out the window. "Look, you've got to make it through this! And I'm sure the child's father will come back someday." The older woman got off at the next stop.

She, too, eventually got off the bus and walked the rest of the way home lost in thought. Calling up the newspaper, she demanded they stop running the ad. Then, she turned off her phone and tossed it into a drawer.

The fetus in her womb, despite having reached peak weight, would occasionally tremble or squirm, but it never kicked or gave her the impression of really being alive. Her anemia worsened. She could see the fetus' movement on the ultrasound but not feel it herself. There wasn't anything particularly wrong with her otherwise. Aside from telling her to hurry up with finding a father, the obstetrician had nothing much to report. She became so large that even other pregnant woman felt uncomfortable in her presence. But what did it mean for the baby to not grow "properly"? She thought of the hostile glare of the obstetrician with the thick make-up. If she needed a father for the baby for its proper growth, what could explain the size of her stomach now? Hadn't she simply been scared by a few words of a doctor—some young woman with a nasty personality? Had she been so focused on finding a father for the baby that she hadn't thought enough about what the baby really needed? Regardless of its growth, whether it had a father or not, the baby was hers and hers alone, in the truest sense. "Live only for the child." Those words didn't completely cleanse her of her worries and anxiety, but she could at long last feel herself calming down as she repeated them.

For the first time in what felt like forever, she felt ravenous. She wanted to eat something delicious for the baby. She jumped up from her seat.

When she opened her eyes again, she was lying on the floor.

Why am I lying here?

She managed to sit up. It took some time for her to gather her wits.

The anemia. I must've fainted when I got up.

She felt around the back of her head. There was a large bump. It began to scare her.

She felt a warmth between her legs.

Did I wet myself when I fainted? This is so embarrassing. I better clean up before my family gets home.

This time, carefully, she got up from the floor. She carefully crossed the apartment to the kitchen, picked up a rag, and slowly wiped the floor with it. The warm water continued to gush as she wiped the floor. A bit of red came up with the rag.

She went to the bathroom. Her underwear was soaked in red. Judging by the smell, the warm liquid was not urine.

It can't be ...

She opened the pregnancy guidebook the obstetrician had given her. "Call the hospital if any of the symptoms below occur." One of the items was "If a clear liquid keeps coming out (if your water broke)."

Her stomach suddenly hurt. The pain ebbed and flowed over her like a rapid tide.

With shaking hands, she called the obstetrician. The back of her head began to throb.

A young nurse picked up the phone, who upon the mention of fainting and anemia and water breaking began to panic. There was now hemorrhaging, and her stomach hurt.

"Look, I'm all alone at home, what do I do? My head keeps hurting from when I bumped it—"

"We're sending an ambulance! It'll be there soon! Don't move, stay on the floor!" The nurse quickly confirmed her name, address, and phone number. "Don't leave your house! The ambulance will be there in a flash!"

The ambulance was indeed there in a flash. The doorbell rang and she opened the door to a group of tall men who rushed in, put her on a gurney, and loaded her onto the ambulance. Another man was standing by outside to help bring the gurney in.

She immediately recognized him. "Um … hey …"

The man's eyes also widened in recognition. He started to say something, but the other men shoved her in before she could hear him. The man quickly shut the door and ran to the driver's seat. He started the engine.

The journey to the hospital was a nightmare. The vehicle shook, the siren was loud, and the paramedics constantly measured, prodded, and questioned her. She had an IV stabbed into her vein, a blood pressure cuff on her arm, and a cold stethoscope traveling across her belly. The back of her head felt like it would split in half from the pain, and she felt a strong urge to throw up. But her labor pains did not return.

Despite the lack of pain, the fetus in her belly was becoming more and more active. As if making up for months of inactivity, it now seemed as if it was about to somersault out of her womb; she could imagine the baby knocking against the walls of her uterus screaming, "I want to be born, I want to live, find me a father!" The paramedics kept asking if she could feel the contractions and at what intervals. She kept answering that she had no contractions and began to fear that there was something wrong with the baby, a fear that became a dark cloud that grew larger and larger and soon enveloped her whole. She grabbed a nearby paramedic and begged him to be the baby's father. Just then, waves of pain overtook her as she moaned and hugged her stomach.

The ambulance suddenly stopped. The driver urgently pressed down on the klaxon.

She shouted the driver's name. She got up from the gurney and crawled toward the driver's seat.

"Please be my baby's father!" she begged her first seon date. "It's not too late! The baby is about to be born! Please help me! It's not too late ..."

The ambulance driver stuck his head out of the driver's seat window and shouted, "Hey, asshole! Get out of the way! This is an ambulance! We've got a pregnant lady with a concussion!"

The paramedics dragged her back onto the gurney and laid her down. The ambulance started moving again. It ran red lights, jumped lanes, and sped past countless cars, zipping by at manic speed. They finally arrived at the hospital, where she was carried out of the ambulance. The man who had been her first seon date restarted the engine and gave her a reluctant last look through the rear-view mirror as she was rolled into the emergency room. The ER confirmed the concussion was fairly light and sent her on to the delivery room.

The delivery waiting room was full of other women with bellies as big as Namsan Mountain, some clinging to their husbands' arms and screaming that they were going to die while others were nonchalantly walking about, quietly sobbing, or conversing with nurses. As for her, the fetus was threatening to burst out at any moment and her body was slowly cracking open with each kick. Pain engulfed her. As it subsided, she was left with a pounding headache that felt like her heart was in her skull. The nurses urged her to walk if she wanted the baby to come out quicker, but her headache was so intense that she couldn't even sit up. She lay in bed and stared up at the ceiling until her eyes became sore from the white fluorescent lights. Her head pounded to the beating of her heart. She felt her head inch away from her body with every beat and slowly float up toward the white ceiling. But it was then yanked back whenever she felt another wave of pain that twisted her like a wet rag. The alternating contractions and headaches lulled her into an eerie sense of calm as her vision was flooded with white light.

The intervals between contractions became shorter and the pain unbearably long and violent. The nurse examined her and said she was ready for the delivery room. Still rising up like a balloon and being jerked back with each wave of pain, she clung to her belly as she walked into the delivery room and hoisted herself upon the delivery table. She could vaguely hear the surreal counting of the doctor as she pushed on cue.

Again. And again. And—

A lump slipped out between her legs, or rather, flowed out. She felt a wonderful relief in her belly.

She lay there quietly, waiting to hear the baby's cries.

Everything was silent.

Neither the doctor nor the nurse moved. No one spoke.

She barely managed to whisper, "What is it? Is it ... dead?"

There was no answer.

"Is the baby dead?"

Terror and despair pierced through her blinding-white senselessness and throttled her. She looked about the room and struggled to sit up. A nurse gently took the baby from the doctor and handed it to her.

The "baby" was a black and red, slightly iron-smelling, enormous blood clot.

"What is this?" she asked as she looked around at the doctor and nurses, propping herself up with one arm and holding the baby with the other. The blood clot against her breast was warm.

"I said, what is this?"

"It's a baby," snapped the obstetrician. Her face was half-covered with a surgical mask, but her bright blue eyeshadow and pitch-black eyeliner were unmistakable.

"This ... this is a baby?"

"I told you to find the baby a father. You were the one who left it to grow without one. This is what you end up with!"

The doctor's voice was cold, and her eyes seemed to say, *This is all your fault.*

The blood clot squirmed.

She flinched.

"The baby is looking for its mother," said the nurse softly, the one who had handed her the "baby." "Now it's looking at the mother. Look back into its eyes."

She could feel the blood clot looking at her as well. But she couldn't tell where exactly the eyes were, or quite frankly, where its head ended and its body began. Confused, she turned the blood clot about, examining it.

The "baby" kept squirming and suddenly began to shudder. The black-red clot very briefly shone transparent and crystalline, like a blood-colored jewel.

The next moment, the "baby" disintegrated into a pool of liquid blood.

Her hand and chest soaked in blood and her arm still curved from when she had held the baby, she stared down mutely at the ruined front of her gown and the puddle of blood in the middle of the delivery table.

The delivery room door slowly opened. Her first seon date, the ambulance driver, hesitatingly entered the chamber.

"You can't be in here," said one of the nurses.

"Oh, I'm ... I'm her guardian. Well. Not yet her guardian, but ..." He turned to her and stammered, "C-could it be possible if I *were* your guardian now? I-I was wondering if it wouldn't be too late ..." His words trailed off as he finally read the room and realized she was covered in blood. "Uh ... that isn't ... ?"

She slowly, mechanically turned her head and stared blankly at the man's confused face. Then she turned, again slowly, with difficulty, to the dripping puddle of blood on the bed that had once been her baby.

She covered her face with her bloody hands and began to cry. Sobs at first, soon escalating into full-on wails. Whether they were tears of relief, sadness from losing the baby, or of something else entirely, she herself couldn't tell.

Cursed Bunny

Grandfather used to say, "When we make our cursed fetishes, it's important that they're pretty."

And the lamp, shaped like a bunny rabbit sitting beneath a tree, is truly pretty. The tree part looks a bit fake, but the bunny was clearly made with love and care. The tips of the bunny's ears and tail are black, as are its eyes, and the body a snowy white. Its material is hard, but its body and pink lips are crafted to look soft to the touch. When the lamp is switched on and the light shines upon it, the bunny looks like it's about to flick its ears or wriggle its nose.

Every object has a story. This object is no exception, especially as it's a cursed fetish. Sitting in an armchair next to the bunny lamp, Grandfather tells me the same story he's already told me time and time again.

The lamp was made for a friend of his.

It is forbidden to make a cursed fetish for personal use. Also according to family tradition, it is forbidden to curse any handmade item. These unwritten rules have been passed down for generations in our family's line of work: the creation of cursed fetishes.

This bunny, however, is the only exception.

"My friend's family were alcoholic spirit artisans," says Grandfather. He always adds, "Do you know what spirit artisans are?"

I know, of course. I've heard this story many times, but Grandfather never gives me a chance to say so.

"You might call his family business a distillery now. Back then, it was the biggest distillery in the region. You can't find a family business that makes such spirits these days, but my friend's family once had a great big factory that employed most of the people in my neighborhood. In those parts, everyone in our community looked up to that spirit artisan family."

Grandfather doesn't remember how the son of such a respected family and himself, whose house made cursed fetishes, became friends. "I don't really recall," he has said to me several times. Grandfather's family, my family in other words, are officially "ironsmiths." We do in fact make or fix farming implements and all sorts of metal things when tasked, but everyone in our neighborhood, down to the little children, knows what our real work is.

Every profession referred to by the polite, contemporary term "occultist"—shamans, fortune-tellers, and morticians—was treated like dirt back then. Such discrimination was far from fair, but that's the way it was. Grandfather's family, or I should say *my* family, were barely afforded the most basic gestures of courtesy. People had no idea what to make of us.

We weren't shamans, we didn't offer exorcism rituals for a price, we couldn't tell people's fortunes, and we were completely unrelated to the business of preparing corpses or the funeral trade. We had something to do with the occult, but no one dared to say out loud what it was, and our ironsmith trade did solid business on the surface. On top of everything else, there was a rumor that we would put a curse on anyone who crossed us. My family would never use a cursed fetish on someone we knew personally, but our neighbors wouldn't have known that, and even if they had, they wouldn't have bothered us, anyways. In any event, we were given a wide berth.

"But my friend did not care about that sort of thing," Grandfather repeatedly insisted. This friend didn't care about the rumors about town, the whispers of the others, the terrified yet curious glances of the neighbors. To the spirit artisan's son, all of the neighborhood children were his friends by default, and he found no reason to not play with someone simply because of their parents' occupation. And because the son of the rich, landed distillery family considered Grandfather a friend, the other children came to accept Grandfather as well.

"His parents were good and wise," Grandfather emphasizes yet again. "They never used their money or power as an excuse to treat others harshly—they bowed as low as anyone else when they greeted their neighbors, and they were always the first to help out with weddings and funerals and such."

This family also happened to be, in today's parlance, innovative entrepreneurs. They had humble beginnings, distilling a batch of spirits whenever they felt like it for their neighbors, and moved on to standardizing and modernizing their production, expanding their sales network nationally. Then, the Korean War. They fled southward like everyone else and returned after the war to find the distillery and neighborhood in ruins. But the family was not disheartened. If anything, they were more determined than ever to use this as an opportunity to start afresh with truly modernized, standardized production.

My grandfather's friend understood his parents' ambitions and inherited them himself.

"We thought he would study business in college because he was going to be the owner, but he specialized in engineering instead. He said he would figure out how to mass produce the taste of wine that was distilled by hand from hard-steamed rice. A nineteen-year-old, fresh out of high school, saying he would conquer the world with his family's spirits! He was all fired up back then."

What threw a wrench into his plans was a new national food policy. At its core was the government's insistence that Korea secure its rice supply, and the use of rice in the fermenting of spirits was subsequently forbidden. The traditional method—of pouring water into a mixture of hard-steamed and malted rice and letting it ferment—was replaced by ethanol, an industrial alcohol, which flooded the market. To make this revolting solution palatable, beverage companies mixed the ethanol with water and artificial flavoring.

My grandfather's friend was devastated. But he didn't give up. He was the last of several generations of skilled distillers, armed with specialized knowledge in this particular area. He accepted the government's stance that rice was precious, that eating it was more important than drinking it. He researched production methods that could restore the old taste by imitating the traditional by-hand methods—the proportion of ingredients, alcohol level, fermentation temperature, and distillation methods—as much as possible within compliance of national policy.

Grandfather always pauses dramatically at this point in the story. "So, what do you think happened after that? Can you guess if he succeeded or failed?"

Again, I've heard the story many times. I already know the answer. But as always, I smile and shake my head.

"He succeeded. He was a smart and steadfast kid." Then, Grandfather smiles sadly. "But then he lost everything."

Grandfather's friend cared only about developing delicious, healthy spirits; he had no idea that in the new, post-war age, connections with government higher-ups, networking, entertaining, and the occasional bribe and backdoor dealing were more important than product quality or technology.

And there was a much larger company that had the transitioning liquor market in their sights, a company that had strong political connections and was skilled in said business-related entertaining. This company had the gall to advertise their mixture of alcohol and artificial flavoring as "a drink for the people" and "the taste of tradition." They ran legitimate ads in newspapers and television while organizing a parallel slander campaign, spreading the lie that the company of my grandfather's friend mixed "industrial-use alcohol" into their beverages. They claimed that anyone who drank it would become blind, lame, or even fatally poisoned.

Sales for my grandfather's friend took a nosedive. His factory ceased operations. No matter how many times his company denied the lies spread by their larger rival, consumers refused to believe them. My grandfather's friend wanted to drink his company's product in front of the cameras to prove how safe it was, but no broadcaster wanted to put him on the air. And there was no internet in those days, nowhere for him to turn to once he was shunned by the newspapers and television. He had no legal recourse because you couldn't record phone conversations or screenshot texts back then—it was impossible to determine how rumors were spread. The courts ruled that there had been no slander or libel, and my grandfather's friend ended up with debts from both his business and the lawsuit. Leaving a note in which he apologized to his family, he hanged himself, still only in his thirties. His wife, who had found the body, fainted several times during the funeral proceedings and would soon join her husband in that place from which they could never return. Their suddenly orphaned children were thankfully taken in by a relative who lived overseas, but that was the last anyone would ever hear from them.

The very company that had spread the lies about "industrial-use alcohol" bought out its ruined competitor at far below market value. The manufacturing processes that my grandfather's friend had devoted his life to developing were also turned over to his competitor, who buried the work in the bottom of a dark vault.

"Why were they buried in a vault?" I naively asked when I first heard this story.

"That evil company's purpose was to sell lots of cheaply made spirits and earn piles of money, not come up with new and better products," explained Grandfather. "And if they're not going to make their products better, they've got to prevent others from doing so if they want to stay competitive."

And that was why Grandfather made the cursed bunny.

"It is no sin to make and sell good spirits. But for the alleged crimes of not being connected to powerful people, for not having the capital to make such connections, an entire family was smashed to pieces and its remains scattered to the winds."

Grandfather shakes his head. "My friend was so good, so kind, so dedicated to his company, and devoted to his wife ... He was such a lovely friend ..." Despite having told this story scores of times, Grandfather's voice always trembles when he gets to this part, his eyes turning red. "To murder them all, to destroy a family ... How can such things be allowed?"

But such things are indeed allowed, and such people who allow it are everywhere. Which is exactly why my grandfather, my father, and I could make a living out of cursed fetishes.

But to my grandfather, I say nothing. As always, I simply listen to his story, so familiar from having heard it many times.

The target of the curse has to touch the cursed fetish with their own hands. That's the most important aspect of any cursed fetish and the trickiest part in getting it to work. Grandfather summoned all his connections, high and low, to get in touch with someone who knew someone who knew yet another someone who worked for a subcontractor for the company that killed his friend. He asked the first someone to hand deliver the bunny lamp to the competitor company's CEO. There was a switch embedded in the back of the bunny that made the light turn on when stroked like a real live pet rabbit.

This someone who knew someone who knew yet another someone did as he was told. He visited the competitor company's CEO and said the lamp was a gift from the subcontractor company, demonstrating the on and off switch with gloved hands. The CEO simply nodded his head, distracted by some papers he was signing, took a call passed on from his assistant, and abruptly left his office saying he had a meeting with a member of the National Assembly.

This someone who knew someone who knew yet another someone had no choice but to leave the bunny lamp behind in the CEO's office. On his way out, he implored the CEO's assistant sitting outside to not let anyone touch the lamp except the CEO, but as he was merely a nobody who worked for a subcontractor, the assistant simply nodded her head like her boss had done and went back to reading her magazine.

Grandfather, having heard what had happened, sighed as it occurred to him that the course of the curse would be altered slightly.

But he figured as long as the cursed bunny was somewhere in the CEO's house or office it wasn't a complete failure.

The bunny lamp stood on a table in the CEO's office for a day until being moved to the company warehouse when the workers were preparing to go home. That night, the bunny nibbled at any paper in the warehouse—cardboard boxes, crumpled newspapers used as packing filler, stacks of old documents, account books going back years, all of it. No one came to the warehouse at night, so the bunny nibbled away undisturbed.

The next morning when the warehouse guard opened the doors, the floor was strewn with bits of paper and rabbit droppings. The guard muttered something about rats and buying rat poison as he cleaned up the mess.

The bunny, still unnoticed in the corner of the warehouse, nibbled at archived papers all through the next night as well. The guard occasionally passed by outside as the bunny munched through the warehouse, and the night watchman also went about as usual with a flashlight in his hand, but the two men only glanced into the small window of the warehouse door; no one could imagine what was happening inside. Once the bunny had chewed up every bit of paper in the warehouse, it started on the wood.

A guard glimpsed something white in the warehouse. It looked like a fluffy bit of cotton, but it disappeared as he approached it. He figured a draft had blown it away. The next day, the little white object had become three, and then six the day after that. The guard thought the retreating white figures seemed to hop just like rabbits, but wild rabbits couldn't possibly be living in that part of the city. He thought nothing of it—there were trucks that needed to be loaded for deliveries to branch offices. The guard, branch worker, truck driver—none of them noticed the white-with-black-tipped-ears-and-tail bunnies that hopped aboard with the crates of alcohol.

Soon after, the warehouses of both the headquarters and the branches, as well as retailers, reported some kind of infestation that resulted in chewed-up paper and wood and pea-sized droppings everywhere. Mousetraps and rat poison were of no use, not even cats helped. Someone glanced at the droppings and remarked that they were too large for rats and looked more like the work of rabbits. The woman who presented this accurate opinion worked as a clerk and had a niece in elementary school who raised rabbits for some kind of nature class, and she had visited the hutch a few times to feed them dried grass. But no one in the branches and no retailers had seen any rabbits inside the warehouse, and the clerk was no rabbit expert, just some woman who spent her days taking inventory and fetching coffee until she would inevitably quit to get married. Everyone ignored her.

The company headquarters and all the branches forced every employee to participate in a rat-catching campaign across the warehouses. Many rats were indeed caught, and the campaign, while leaving the workers exhausted, did result in cleaner warehouses. But all it took was another night for the warehouse floors to be littered with shredded paper as well as animal droppings too big to be from rats.

As paper kept getting damaged, the company decided to move their most important documents, like old account books and factory blueprints, to their offices. While they did so, no one noticed that the white bunnies with black-tipped ears and tails, invisible under the daylight sun, were also moving into the office.

A rumor spread that the distillery was overrun with mice.

As so much of the local population worked across the company—at the headquarters, branches, warehouses, and the factory—it was inevitable that word got out in the area.

One branch fired a warehouse worker as a warning while another division brought all of their workers together in one room and begged them to be careful about spreading rumors. The dismissed worker happened to be taking care of his old, bedridden mother as well as three sons and five younger siblings, and he was later caught by the night watchman when he broke into the warehouse with a container full of gasoline to set fire to the place. Meanwhile, in the region where they had gathered workers to lecture them on spreading rumors, a full-page opinion piece appeared in the local newspaper about the dangers of rats when it came to food sanitation.

News about the "rat" problem spread like wildfire all over the region, and the company decided to host a tasting event when they determined they were past the point where threatening their workers was effective. They came up with a plan where workers and their families, people who lived near the facilities, and most importantly, the pillars of the community and other important persons of the region were plied with spirits from the warehouse and shown how there was no problem with the sanitation or quality of their product and how much the company was contributing to the local community.

The event was held on the lawns of the headquarters. The CEO himself attended, as did his son the vice-president who had a child in elementary school. The CEO's grandson, bored with the long speeches, the loud music, and most of all the drinking the adults were indulging in, slipped away to wander around the company grounds. The CEO's daughter-in-law found him crouched before an open door of the warehouse. "I was playing with the bunnies." She asked where they were. The boy dragged her into the warehouse by the hand. He pointed at a bunny lamp perched on top of a dusty steel filing cabinet and begged her to let him take it home.

His mother said they needed to ask his grandfather because the object belonged to the company, and she quickly forgot about it as she dragged her son back to the outdoor event. But the boy didn't forget. His drunk grandfather, upon hearing what the boy said to him about wanting a strange object in the warehouse, told him to go ahead before turning back to drinking with the important adults.

The PR event was a success. Everyone stayed late, drinking the free alcohol into the wee hours of the night. Having endured it for as long as she could, the CEO's daughter-in-law left with the child when he began whining from exhaustion. The boy hugged the bunny lamp tightly in the car that took him home.

The "rat" rumor seemed like it had finally been laid to rest, and the fundamental reason for the rumors—the bunny lamp—had been moved from the warehouse to the house of the CEO's son.

But the bunnies that had already spread throughout the company's branches and retailers' warehouses did not go away. The ones that had moved into the offices with the documents didn't go away either. They continued to multiply and chew up everything in sight.

Every night inside the drawers and steel cabinets, all manner of documents—order forms, contracts, business performance reviews, account books, and financial statements—were chewed to shreds.

Even when the most important documents were moved into the vault, the cash, cheques, and promissory notes within began to get chewed up as well.

The company undertook a building-wide professional extermination, dumping all of their things on the lawns including the contents of the vault. As all this went on, the CEO's grandson did his homework by the light of the bunny lamp at home and slept in a bed right next to it. The boy loved the cute lamp of the bunny sitting beneath a tree and bragged to his friends that his grandfather had been gifted it from overseas. The CEO's grandson touched the lamp several times a day, stroking the bunny's back in order to switch the light on and off.

The bunny did not chew up the paper in the house of the CEO's son.

It chewed up something else instead.

The CEO's grandson was in his last year of elementary school. Aside from being smaller than average for his age, he was a strong boy with no history of illness. According to his mother, he was a nice enough child who enjoyed going to school and did well in his studies, albeit a little too enthusiastic about kicking a ball around instead of doing his homework or cramming for exams.

No one paid much attention at first when he began to forget his homework and school materials. He was the grandson of the brewery owner and had always been a good student; the teacher didn't scold him so much as nag him. But the child soon began to forget not only his homework but the fact that he had been assigned it in the first place, and in a burst of irritation he lashed out at his teacher, prompting a call home. "Please keep in mind that children enter puberty early these days and can get moody," the teacher said to the mother, and the mother acquiesced.

Around the end of winter vacation, the boy began obsessing over food. He insisted he hadn't eaten when he clearly had, stole food from the fridge, hid snacks around the house, and threw screaming fits when his mother tried to take the food away. His family assumed it was because he was a growing boy. Thinking he might be going through a growth spurt, they bought more food, and a greater variety at that, but the boy's greed, paranoia, and temper only worsened.

Then, on the first day of school in the spring, the boy got lost on his way home. It was the same path he had walked every school day for the past six years, a distance he could cover in ten minutes, fifteen at most.

A neighbor found him sitting in the middle of the road, dazed from having wandered around the vicinity of the school for a long time. The boy smelled terrible. The neighbor who brought him to his mother, embarrassedly mentioned that the boy seemed to have soiled his pants, and she turned around and quickly walked away before the boy's mother could even recover from the shock and thank her.

The boy's parents took him to see a doctor. Their local pediatrician recommended they take him to a larger hospital.

But even the university hospital in the city could not find anything wrong, this being a time before MRI scans. The pediatrician at the university hospital did observe, however, that the child's eyes seemed unfocused as he rocked back and forth mumbling unintelligibly, and that he had peed himself where he sat. The doctor recommended consulting a psychiatrist. His chair fell on its side as the child's father jumped to his feet and cried, "Are you suggesting my son is mad!" His face turning crimson, the father screamed the most wretched curses at the doctor as he pushed aside his pleading wife and swept up his child in his arms before leaving the hospital. The blameless mother tearfully begged the doctor for his forgiveness as she bowed several times before following her husband out.

The child's condition only grew worse after their visit to the university hospital. The child could no longer recognize his parents' faces, repeatedly soiled his trousers, could not walk properly, and kept muttering to himself but no longer formed meaningful words. He spent most of his day lying in bed and staring up at the ceiling with unfocused eyes, gurgling now and then, but the one thing he consistently did was obsess over the bunny lamp. The bunny lamp was moved from his desk to his nightstand, and the child, while mumbling at the ceiling, turned to look at the lamp from time to time, which seemed to reassure him, and he became anxious and screamed whenever anyone else tried to touch it.

While he slept, the child would sometimes wriggle his nose, nibble, or flick his ears like a bunny, but none of the adults around him noticed. In his dreams, the child sat under a tree with a white rabbit with black-tipped ears and tail, pleasantly eating away at his own brain. The more he nibbled away at it, the narrower the child's world became until he was unable to leave the little bit of land he shared under the tree with the bunny. By then, he could not comprehend anything except for his delight in being with his friend.

As the CEO's grandson slowly died on the bed next to the bunny lamp, the seasons changed, as did the government and the world. The people who had enabled the CEO to monopolize the liquor market with his cheap and tasteless spirits lost their positions of power. The company, for the first time since its founding, was hit with a tax audit.

By that point, the invisible bunnies had shredded the company's performance reviews, account books, financial statements, and daily memorandums. Every operating profit notification, every record of taxes paid to the National Tax Service, everything was in pieces and completely illegible.

The bunnies had moved on to the wallpaper of the office building, leaving teeth marks on the walls and doors. The company's important documents were now nothing but a pile of hamster bedding, and the building itself began to look shabby. It was clear to the workers that the company, both inside and out, was falling apart. But the CEO refused to acknowledge this and continued to turn a blind eye.

For a long time, the CEO's grandson lay in bed staring up at the ceiling with unfocused eyes, breathing and doing nothing else.

Then one day, the child stopped breathing.

Returning home from the elaborate funeral they'd held for his son, the father locked himself in his dead son's room and wept for a long time. He placed the bunny lamp his son had loved so much on his lap and wailed his son's name again and again as he stroked it.

The National Tax Service determined that the company not only had to pay back all the taxes it had skillfully avoided in the past but even the taxes it had actually paid, plus interest. No matter how desperately the company tried to prove they had paid the latter, the company didn't have a single legible document to submit as evidence.

When whispers began that the company's operations and financial documents had vanished, its debtors insisted there was no proof they owed the company anything and refused to make payments. At the same time, the company's creditors demanded they pay up immediately. The CEO was livid. He went to a secret safe where he kept a notebook that only he knew about, a record of all of the company's assets and bonds and debt documents. But when he opened the safe, he found his trusted secret notebook torn to shreds, chewed to pieces—a pile of useless pulp.

This should have been the moment when the CEO had a stroke and never regained consciousness. The cursed bunny, however, was not that generous. The CEO did not have a stroke.

It was the CEO's son who had the stroke. After the man had cried himself to sleep on his dead son's bed, he woke up the next morning, put a foot down on the floor ... and promptly broke his right ankle. As he fell, he flung out his left arm to protect his head, breaking it in three places along with sustaining a hairline crack.

The CEO's son was barely forty, a healthy adult man. He had never had a serious injury in his life, nor had he ever broken a bone before.

As the CEO's son lay in bed with large casts on his right leg and left arm after the bones had metal rivets surgically screwed into them, the company began to deteriorate at a rapid rate. The CEO was so busy running, both away from his creditors and after his debtors, that he didn't even have time to visit his only son in the hospital. The CEO's son anxiously interrogated his wife about the goings-on of the company, and determining that he couldn't just lay there as the company fell apart, he tried to get up from the bed. But the moment he put his undamaged left foot on the floor, it broke. He fell over and fractured his tailbone.

The subsequent operation took nine whole hours. Afterwards, he was brought back to his hospital room where, under the influence of anesthesia, he rested motionless for a long time save for the occasional nose-wriggling and nibbling motion of his lips.

The bunny nibbled away.

The CEO finally came to see his son in the hospital on the day the company went bankrupt. Like a mummy, his son was almost completely wrapped in bandages and fast asleep thanks to the tranquilizers.

When he woke from anesthesia the first time, he mumbled something about a rabbit sitting on the bed. At first, no one took his words seriously. The CEO's son insisted that there was a rabbit sitting on the bed, eating away at his blanket. No one took that seriously, either. The CEO's son finally yelled that the rabbit was eating his feet, and he tried to jump out of bed. His bewildered wife called for help, and a group of nurses rushed in and tried to restrain him. The man resisted, shouting something incomprehensible about bunnies. Two nurses held down his arms and his wife hugged his torso. That was how his right arm broke and two of his ribs got cracked.

After that, every time he opened his eyes the CEO's son screamed about bunnies, and his bones would break each time they restrained him. They broke when the people trying to help pinned him down, they broke when he banged his hand against his headboard or struggled against his casts. The only way to allow him to recover was to keep him constantly sedated.

The CEO stared at the bandage-wrapped face of his unresponsive son, who was locked in insensate despair. His precious grandson was already dead, and his sole heir, a son who was third in a generational line of only sons, had become this worthless, broken lump. The company was gone, and all he was left with was debt—the unpaid taxes and fines, his loans, and his son's hospital fees. He couldn't take his son out of the hospital when his bones shattered at the slightest touch. And it would all be over if he himself ended up in jail for tax evasion.

Grandfather stops the story and stares into the lamp. The bunny underneath the tree is plump, with fur that is white except for the tips of its black ears and tail. It's made of a hard material, but the luminous bunny next to Grandfather seems covered in soft fur, its ears about to twitch and its mouth about to make nibbling motions.

"So what happened next?" I ask. Of course, I know what happens next. The questions I ask when the storytelling stops in the expected places aren't questions per se, but prompts for him to go on with the story, unwritten stage directions we have more or less come to agree upon.

"They all died," says Grandfather, absently stroking the ears and head of the bunny. "The CEO's son died in the hospital, a funeral was held, and the next day, the CEO himself fell from the roof of his company building."

The bunny flicks the tip of its ears.

Never make a cursed fetish for personal reasons. Never use a handmade object in a personal curse. There are reasons for these unwritten rules.

There's a Japanese saying that goes, "Cursing others leads to two graves." Anyone who curses another person is sure to end up in a grave themselves.

Although in Grandfather's case, there are more than two graves: the CEO he cursed, the CEO's son, and the CEO's grandson. All dead. And to this day, no one knows the location of Grandfather's grave. He just left home one day and never returned.

Well, no. I suppose he did return.

On evenings when the moon is covered by gloomy clouds, or when it's raining so heavily that the showers seem to obscure the light of the streetlamps, or on nights so dark and forlorn that no light neither natural nor artificial can withstand it, Grandfather reappears in the armchair next to the window, turns on the bunny lamp, and begins to tell the same story he has told me scores of times before.

Perhaps that's Grandfather's curse.

Or, his blessing.

"It's late," he says, "you've got to sleep early if you want to go to school tomorrow."

I am well past school-attending age. No one in this house goes to school anymore. But I always answer the same way.

"Yes, Grandfather. Good night."

Then, on impulse, I give his wrinkled cheek a light peck.

There was a time when I wondered if I should ask how he died, what happened to his body, or where his grave is. I've thought about it several times. But now I firmly suppress the desire to ask whenever it threatens to get a hold of me.

If Grandfather ever remembers how he died, he might stop coming. Worse, he might not remember, leaving my questions unanswered, and his surprise at my questions may make him disappear for good. I couldn't stand it if that happened.

So I say nothing. I quietly turn around, go back to my room, and close the door.

But not completely. I leave it open a crack to see Grandfather still sitting in the armchair and the pretty bunny lamp shining next to him. The sight reassures me.

"When we make our cursed fetishes, it's important that they're pretty."

That's what my grandfather used to say. And business is better than ever these days.

If I keep doing the work that I'm doing now, I'll end up like Grandfather. Dead but not dead, sitting in the dark of some living room on a moonless night in front of an object that keeps me anchored to the world of the living.

But by the time I sit at that armchair by the window, there will be no child or grandchild to listen to my story. And in this twisted, wretched life of mine, that single fact remains my sole consolation.

I close the door and walk down the hall into complete darkness.

The Frozen Finger

She opens her eyes.

Darkness. Pitch black. Like someone has dropped a thick veil of black over her eyes. Not even a pinpoint of light to be seen.

Has she gone blind?

She tries moving a hand in front of her face. There does seem to be a faint object there. But nothing she can clearly discern.

After a few more attempts at this, she gives up. The darkness is simply too dense.

What hour could be so dark? And where in the world ...

She extends her arm and probes the space before her. A round thing. Solid.

A steering wheel.

She slips her right hand behind the wheel. The ignition. Her keys are still in it. She turns them. No response. The engine is dead.

Her left hand prods the left side of the wheel. It grips something that feels like a hard stick. She pulls it down. The left-arrow on the dashboard should have lit up. No light to be seen. She pushes it down. Still no light. She feels her way to the tip of the lever and turns the headlight switch. And of course, the lights do not turn on.

What has happened?

She tries to remember. But her memories are as dark as the scene before her.

"—eacher."

A woman's voice, thin and frail. She looks up. The voice calls for her again.

"Teacher."

Craning her head toward the voice, she strains her ears attempting to determine where it's coming from. But the voice is so thin that its direction is unclear.

"Teacher Lee."

"Yes?" she answers. She can't make out where the voice is coming from, who is speaking—or whether the voice is in fact calling for *her*. But the sound of another person's voice in the darkness is such a relief that she finds herself answering before she can stop herself.

"Are you there? Who are you? I'm over here!"

"Teacher Lee, are you all right?" The voice is coming from the left. "Teacher Lee, are you hurt?"

She tries moving her arms and legs. No pain anywhere in particular. "No."

The thin voice, still coming from the left, says, "Then come out of the car, quickly."

"Why? What happened? Where am I?"

"We're in a swamp," the thin voice patiently explains, "and

the car is sinking, little by little. I think you better come out of there."

She tries to get up. The safety belt presses down on her torso. Tracing the belt to her waist, she presses the release and the safety belt disengages. She turns to the left and gropes around for the door handle. There, the glass pane of the window. More prodding, downward.

"Teacher, you must hurry."

The door handle. She pulls it. The door doesn't move. She pushes it.

"Teacher Lee, hurry!"

"The door won't open."

She doesn't know what to do.

The thin voice commands, "It's locked from the inside. You must unlock it."

Feeling around the door handle again, she can feel the protrusions of buttons; she presses them, one by one. At the third button, she hears a *clunk*. The brief vibration felt through the door is as welcome as the Savior Himself.

She pulls at the door handle again. The door seems to open little by little. But it's blocked by something.

"The door won't open," she says, pushing it with her shoulder.

From right beside her, the thin voice says, "That's because the car is lodged in mud. Let me help you."

Someone's finger brushes against her hand that's pushing the door. The door opens a little more.

"Quickly. Get out of there," says the thin voice.

Doing as the voice commands, she brings her left leg out

of the car first before suddenly remembering something.

"Wait ... wait a second."

She crouches down in the seat and starts to grope around beneath the steering wheel. The long thing on the right is the accelerator, the wide thing on the left is the brake. She stretches her right hand into the space below the pedals. She can feel the scratchy mat and the mud smeared on it. Of the thing she is searching for, nothing.

"What are you doing? You must get out of there immediately!" The thin voice is getting anxious.

"Just wait ..."

Extending her hand even further beneath the seat, she feels a long, thin steel rod. It's probably the lever that adjusts the driver's seat, moving it back and forth. She feels underneath it. Again, just the mat and mud, plus a little dust.

She can feel her left leg, the one that made it outside the car, slowly start to rise. The car door begins to close with it, putting pressure on her left leg.

The voice shouts, "Teacher Lee, hurry! I don't know what you're looking for, but just leave it and come out!"

"But ... but ..." She can't bring herself to say it.

"But what? What is it?"

"Something very important ..." Her voice trails off.

She touches her left hand with her right. There's no ring on her left ring finger. Her hands feel about the driver's seat where she's sitting, then the passenger side.

"What could be so important? What is it?" the thin voice asks again.

Her left hand grabbing the frame of the car, she stretches

her right arm as far as she can to beneath the passenger-side seat.

"A ring ..."

Her hand can't reach as far as the other seat; all she can grasp are the gearshift and handbrake. She manages to stretch her arm a little further. There's no one in the passenger-side seat. Perhaps because of her odd posture, her hand can't quite reach the bottom of the other seat.

The finger from before touches her left hand again.

"This. Is this what you're talking about?"

A small, round, and hard object against her skin. Someone's fingers slip it onto the ring finger of her left hand.

She sits up and touches her left hand with her right. It's still impossible to see, but the smooth touch and the slightly uncomfortable thickness pressing against her fingers feels familiar.

"Is this it?" asks the thin voice.

"Yes. How did you—"

"This is it, right? Come out, quick. It's dangerous," says the thin voice urgently.

With her right hand, she pushes the slowly closing door. She barely manages to squeeze the left side of her body out the door.

"Be careful," warns the thin voice. "The ground outside isn't solid."

Her left foot lands on the ground with a *plop*. She shoves the car door with her left hand and the car frame with her right, slowly getting out of the car.

With every step, her feet sink into the ground. It's hard to keep her balance. Just as she's about to stumble, the frozen fingers grab onto her left hand.

"Be careful. One step at a time, slowly."

Doing as the voice instructs, she takes one tentative step at a time, moving further and further away from the car.

Suddenly, she stops.

"What's wrong?" asks the voice.

"Did you ... hear something?"

"Hear what?" the voice asks again.

"Someone ... I thought there was someone there."

The thin voice is silent, as if pausing to listen. Then, it says, "You're mistaken. There's only the two of us here."

She listens again.

The sound is vague. Somewhat far away in the distance, or right by her ear, something like a human voice, or the wind ...

The sound withers into silence.

"I'm so sure there was someone there—"

"There's no one here except us," the voice says adamantly. "If you think you heard something, it might have been wild animals." The fingers gripping her left hand give a squeeze. "I think ... we should run away from here."

The voice sounds afraid.

Fear seeps from her fingers through her hand, moving up her arm and into her heart.

Wordlessly, she begins to walk.

Her feet occasionally sink into the unstable ground, almost making her fall. Whenever that happens, the fingers, gripping her left hand so hard that it hurts, hold her steady and help her find her balance.

There is no way of knowing where they are going. Nor of determining where they are. But the thin voice sounds as frightened as she feels, and the fingers that grasp her left hand feel dependable. And so, she decides to believe in the voice and fingers as they walk together over the pitch-black ground into which their feet sink, going further into the unknown.

"Ah, here we go," the voice says, reassured. "The ground is firmer here."

That moment, her left foot lands on firm ground. Then, her right.

"It's so much easier to walk," says the voice, delighted.

"Shall we rest a bit?" she suggests. Walking endlessly through mud into which her feet keep sinking was exhausting for both the body and soul.

Without waiting for an answer, she sits down on the road. The owner of the thin voice sits down next to her. She can't see her, but she can sense her sitting down.

"That ring. It must be very important?" the thin voice asks carefully.

She fondles the round, hard, and smooth object on the ring finger of her left hand.

"Well ... yes."

The thin voice asks again, still careful. "Is it ... really that important?"

"Well ... I mean ..."

Her hand keeps touching the ring finger.

A large, warm hand, memories of that hand wrapped around her own, a familiar face she was always glad to see, such pleasure, such happiness ... Something like that. An important, precious something, like ...

But the more she tries to recall these memories the fainter they become, and like the last rays of the setting sun, they disappear leaving just a trace of their warmth behind. The only thing left in her mind is that which has ruled her and surrounded her since the moment she opened her eyes: the darkness.

As she keeps silent, the thin voice apologizes.

"I'm sorry, I didn't mean to pry—"

"Oh ... it's fine."

She is beginning to feel like something is wrong.

"I just ... I can't remember ... My mind is so dark—"

"Oh no. Are you hurt?" The thin voice sounds worried.

"But ... I'm not sick at all."

"Let me see."

She can feel the fingers touch her forehead and scalp.

"Does this hurt?" asks the thin voice.

"No."

The fingers tap her temples. "What about here?"

"It's fine—"

"Oh no ..." The voice sighs lightly. "We should get out of here quick and go to a hospital as soon as possible."

She touches her own head and face. There doesn't seem to be any wounds, and she doesn't feel any bleeding. There is only the darkness that permeates her mind.

"Um ... excuse me," she says after touching her face and head for a bit. "Where ... where are we? What happened to us?"

"Oh my, you don't remember?" The voice seems surprised.

"Not a thing," she answers listlessly.

"We went to Teacher Choi and her new husband's housewarming party and got into an accident on the way back … You really don't remember?"

"No."

Nothing, she remembers nothing. She turns the inside of her head upside down, looking for something. All she finds is darkness and yet more darkness.

"Uh, Teacher …" The thin voice sounds uncertain. "Then you … you don't remember who I am, do you?"

She hesitates. She wants to cry. "I don't."

"Oh my, what are we to do …" The thin voice becomes even thinner, as if sapped of strength. "I'm Teacher Kim … in the class next to yours, Grade 6 Class 2 … You don't remember?"

"I'm not sure." *So "Teacher" meant elementary school teacher,* she thinks to herself.

The thin voice becomes urgent. "Teacher Choi, she taught Grade 5 with us, and then quit after getting married … She followed her husband out of Seoul. You were invited to their housewarming, so you came along… You really don't remember?"

"I don't know."

"This really is serious." The fingers touch her left hand again. Like before, their grip is firm. "We should get up."

"What?" She is up on her feet before she knows it.

The thin voice is adamant. "Teacher Lee, I think your injuries are more serious than we realize. We shouldn't waste any more time—we should get up and find a hospital."

"Oh."

"Are you very tired?"

"What? Oh, no, not—"

"Then let's go." The fingers gently tug at her left hand.

She begins to follow.

As she walks, she asks, "So, how did we get into this accident?"

The thin voice sighs. "I don't know either ... I drank too much, which is why you were driving."

"Oh." Her guilt blocks her words for a while. After a pause, she asks again. "Then that ... that car. Is it yours, Teacher Kim?"

The voice doesn't answer.

Feeling rebuffed, she stops asking questions.

But after walking in silence for a moment, she can't help asking again. "Where ... where can we be, do you think?"

"Well ..." The voice seems reluctant to answer.

She persists. "Teacher Choi's house, where is it exactly? Is it close to here?"

"Well, the thing is, I don't know either ... I fell asleep as soon as we left ..." The voice's answer trails off.

She thinks a bit more.

She asks, "Do you happen to have a phone?"

The voice does not answer for a moment. Then, "A phone? No. Do you have one, Teacher Lee?"

"I don't either."

The voice asks, "Did you not look for it when you were searching for your ring?"

Sensing a shade of reproach, she answers, "There was nothing in the front seats ... What about the back?"

"It was too dark to look. It could've flown out the window." But the voice seems uncertain.

The conversation stops again.

She has no idea how long they've been walking since leaving the car behind. All around them, it is still complete darkness. No risen moon, no stars. *How long do we have to wait until daybreak*, she wonders.

"Where ... where exactly are we going?" she tentatively asks.

The voice doesn't answer.

She asks again. "Do you ... do you even know where we're headed?"

For a moment, the voice doesn't speak. Then, instead of answering her question: "Teacher Choi, I feel sorry for her."

"Excuse me?" She's taken aback.

The thin voice mumbles as if it isn't meant for her to hear. "So happy when she got married, like the whole world belonged to her, but then divorced within a year, quitting her job at the school ..."

She waits. But the voice does not continue.

So she asks again. "Um ... what are you talking about?"

The thin voice mumbles again. "It's not her fault that her husband had an affair ... Don't you think it's unfair? They say a teacher must always set an example, but she's a woman, after all. A divorced woman, at that ..."

"What are you talking about ... Didn't you just say Teacher Choi was a newlywed?"

The thin voice laughed a thin laugh. "I suppose she is, if it was only a year ago she got married—"

"But, just now, you said Teacher Choi just got married, we were at their housewarming party …"

"Oh Teacher Lee, you must've hit your head rather hard." Patiently, the thin voice explains. "Teacher Choi got divorced, went alone down to the countryside, and we were visiting her in her new room, as both a housewarming and consolation …"

After a moment of silence, the thin voice starts mumbling again. "Living alone turned her into such a lush, all that drinking she did …"

She is flummoxed. "But, but—"

"You really don't remember anything?" says the thin voice. Then, muttering, "Oh my goodness, we really ought to take you to the hospital, quick."

The words make her shut her mouth.

There are no more words as they keep on walking.

She stares at the sky as she walks. It is so dark that she has no idea whether what she is looking at is, indeed, the sky. She thinks of how she has never known such a darkness before in her life. If she has indeed been in a car crash, that would mean she'd been on a road, but how can there not be a single streetlamp?

Where is she? And where is she walking to?

"Teacher Choi, such a shame …" The thin voice, walking in front of her, is speaking again.

She doesn't answer.

"Her mother, she kept crying … She was so young, and to die so horrifically—"

Interrupting sharply, "What are you talking about?"

The thin voice sighs. "You saw it, too, Teacher Lee, at the funeral ... Oh, right, you said you don't remember."

Hearing a mocking tone at the trailing end of the voice's reply, she fiercely counters with, "Why are you talking about a funeral? You said it was a housewarming, earlier—"

"You really must have hit your head hard." The thin voice tsk-tsked. "I understand if you like someone for a long time, but to kill yourself over a crush ... So young at that, the poor family—"

"Didn't you ... didn't you say Teacher Choi was married?" she says, forcing her trembling voice to sound firm. "That her husband had an affair, that she got divorced ... Isn't that what you said?"

The thin voice lets out a thin breath.

"Whew ... What on earth are you going on about ... You should know better by now."

"But you said so earlier. You said it was Teacher Choi's housewarming as a newlywed, then it was her room ... You said she was married, then she was divorced ..."

"Teacher Lee, you're talking in circles. Does your head hurt a lot?"

She shuts her mouth.

"Teacher Choi ... such a pathetic tale, don't you think?" mumbles the thin voice after a pause. "Even with those rose-colored glasses of hers, you would think she'd seen how blatantly her man was getting it on with the teacher in the next class. The whole school knew about it, but she was really stubborn in her denial ... Then when that other woman stole her man, she quit teaching and kicked up that whole fuss about killing herself ..." The thin voice briefly pauses.

She waits.

"Then she really killed herself ..."

She can't tell whether the thin voice is suppressing a sob or a laugh.

She feels a sharp pain as the brief but intense trust she felt for the thin voice is torn in two. Fear digs into her heart. Carefully, she steps aside a little to the right. The thin voice from her left keeps mumbling as if she isn't there.

"Life, really, is so unfair. Everyone is born the same way, but some steal husbands, others are sucked dry and spat out like used chewing gum ..."

She doesn't answer.

The thin voice keeps talking. "Isn't it funny? Two people are in the same car accident, but one lives to tell the tale, the other dies on the spot—"

"You. Who are you?" She cannot suppress the shaking in her voice anymore.

The thin voice casually goes on. "Don't you think it's so unfair? Alone when alive, and still alone when dead."

"Where is this place?" she shrieks. "What's happened to me?!"

The thin voice on her left gives a thin cackle. "People, you know, they're so funny. Don't you think? Just because they're afraid, they go about trusting in any old voice they hear around them, even when they can't see for the life of them."

"What are you?" She is shouting now. "Wh-where is this? Where are you taking me?"

The thin voice continues to cackle. "Following a strange voice around in a strange place, just because it pretends to be kind …"

She cannot stand it anymore. She begins to run.

The voice keeps cackling behind her and mumbling. "She doesn't even know who she is, or where she's going …"

She runs. She doesn't know where she's going but feels some relief at how the voice seems to be getting farther away, and so she keeps blindly running.

The ground beneath her feet suddenly caves in. She stumbles momentarily. After a bit of flailing she rights herself, and a bright light suddenly fills her vision. Her eyes, so used to the dark, lose all their function in the sudden glare. She freezes in the flood of light.

For a brief second, she sees clearly straight ahead—her own self sitting in a car that's lost control, barreling toward her, her expression frozen in fear, her hands ineffectually grasping the steering wheel where a third set of five fingers, mockingly casual, are holding the wheel between her two hands.

Then, darkness again.

"—eacher."

A woman's voice, thin and frail. She opens her eyes. The voice calls for her again.

"Teacher."

It's the voice again. She tries to turn her head to the direction the voice is coming from. Her neck, however, doesn't move.

"Teacher Lee."

Before she can speak, a familiar voice answers.

"Yes?"

Hearing her own voice answer the thin voice, she feels like her whole body is convulsing underneath the car. But her body doesn't move. A slimy mud, or something that is like mud but nothing she can ever know for sure, is making its sticky, stubborn, and ominous way over her ankles to her knees, thighs, stomach, slowly but ceaselessly crawling up the rest of her body.

She can hear conversation from afar.

"Are you there? Who are you? I'm over here!"

"Teacher Lee, are you all right?"

She tries with all of her might. Her right arm is pinned down beneath a wheel. She just about manages to free her left hand. It grips the bumper. Trying to pull herself from underneath the car, she puts all her strength into her left arm.

Suddenly, cold fingers touch her left hand. She makes a fist. But it's too late. The cold fingers have wrested the round, hard, and smooth ring from her hand.

"No ..." She tries to shout it. But her voice has crawled down her throat.

The thin voice whispers into her ear, "You've been hurt badly, you really shouldn't move. Tea. Cher. Lee." It cackles softly as it moves away from her ear.

She feels slight vibrations from the car that covers her.

"Be careful. One step at a time, slowly."

It's the thin voice, from a distance.

She opens her mouth. With all her strength, with all the fear and rage and despair pooled in her heart, she screams.

"What's wrong?" she can hear the voice ask.

"Did you ... hear something?"

"Hear what?" the voice asks again.

"Someone ... I thought there was someone there ..."

She can just about hear heavy footsteps coming down on soft ground. The conversation becomes more and more distant.

The car sinks. She hears the sound of bones breaking somewhere in her body. Strangely enough, the sound makes her realize she no longer feels pain.

All she can feel is the enormous weight of the car as it drags her down into the unknown abyss.

Snare

This is a story I once read long ago.

Once upon a time, a man walking through snow-covered mountain forests came across a fox struggling in a snare. The fox's fur meant money, and the man, thinking he would kill the fox for her fur, approached the animal with a knife in hand.

The fox then lifted her head and spoke in a human voice, "Please let me go."

The man was taken aback. At the same time, he noticed that from the fox's ankle where the snare dug in, a shining liquid flowed. The fox bled not blood but something that resembled gold. The surrounding snow had made it hard to notice at first, but now he saw the area around the snare was splattered with the glittering substance, some of it hardened in the cold snow.

The man picked up one of the hardened lumps and peered at it closely. He bit down on it.

Gold. It was unmistakable.

Taking great care, the man assiduously scraped up every bit that was around the fox. Then, with even more care, he packed the fox inside his bag, someone else's snare and all, and took her home.

Once home, the man hid away the fox deep in his shed. He gave the fox water and food, keeping it alive. The snare was never taken off. Rather, the man would occasionally shake the snare or wound the fox again with a sharp weapon so that her injuries never healed. Whenever he did so, the fox barked or whined in resentment. But the only time she spoke like a human was when the man had first discovered her.

The man let the liquid that flowed from her wounds set before selling it little by little. Cunning as he was, he knew very well what would happen if a peasant like him suddenly showed up with fistfuls of gold in his pockets. He deliberately carried small dribbles of it instead of big ones, going from town to town, selling so little as to never attract much attention. With the money from the gold he sold, he bought grains, salt, leather, and timber—ordinary goods that he could sell in his own village's market.

There were days when business was good and days when it was bad. The price of goods went down sometimes, up in others. But the man didn't care. In his shed at home was a hidden treasure that nobody knew about; never again would he have to start over from nothing. Whether he made a good profit or a small one, he always had a leisurely smile on his face, successfully selling all manner of things at the market.

The people around him considered the man an easy-going

and hardworking fellow. His reputation grew among both his customers and the people who provided him with his wares. Like everyone else, he seemed to have ups and downs with his business, but the thing about this man's work in particular was that he always managed to turn a profit in the end. He became known as an old hand in the art of market-selling. His credit grew as did his fortune, and the man eventually built a large house and married a beautiful woman.

When he built the house, the man knocked down his shed and erected a sturdy warehouse instead, keeping the fox chained to a corner of it. Her constantly open wound and her blood being drawn at regular intervals made her listless, but she was still alive. The skin around the wound, having been ground down and cut again and again, had peeled back to reveal the bone, and was now so calloused that no amount of cutting and piercing drew blood. Now skin and bone, the fox would snarl at the man whenever he came toward her, but that was all she could do. She had long lost the energy to bark or bite.

In the third year of the man's marriage, the fox finally died. The man regretted it deeply, but because he had extracted so much gold from her and business was going well, he thought he would be able to get by. He skinned the dead fox and had her fur made into a scarf. The fox had lost much of its hair during her imprisonment and her fur was not much to look at anymore, but the man's ignorant wife was happy to receive the fox-fur scarf as a gift.

Not long after that, the man's wife became pregnant. As they had been childless for the three years since their wedding, both man and wife were overjoyed at the prospect of a child. Ten months later, the man's wife gave birth to twins: a son and a daughter. The boy came out first, the girl second. Gazing at the faces of their new-born children, the man and his wife felt they had reached the pinnacle of all happiness under heaven.

Aside from the fact that they were fraternal twins, the two children were not that different from most siblings. But one day, around the time they were learning how to walk, the man's wife suddenly heard one of them scream in the other room. When she ran in, she saw that the boy was attacking the girl, biting her. Thinking it was a common fight between siblings, the man's wife separated the two and scolded the boy while consoling the girl. She was too concerned with the wound on the girl's neck to notice that the boy was busily licking away at the blood underneath his fingernails and around his mouth, as if trying to lap up every drop of it.

In the evening, the wife fed her children and put them to bed before letting the man know about the children's fight when he came home. As she was telling the man, they heard another bloodcurdling scream. The couple rushed into the children's room. As the little girl shook in fear and struggled to get free with all her might, the boy bit into the wound scratched onto his sister's neck earlier that day, clawing at it with his little fingernails and rapidly licking away at the blood that flowed from her neck.

The man's wife got in between them and held her daughter away from the son. Jumping at her, the boy bit down on his mother's arm. She was taken by surprise, but despite her pain she kept her daughter aloft and reflexively shoved the boy away. Her fingernail grazed his forehead.

As the man tried to keep his son from his wife, he noticed something glistening on his son's forehead.

Oozing out of the long wound was a familiar glob of gold-colored liquid.

His wife tried to console their bleeding daughter as the man held onto his son and probed his son's wound with his fingers. The wound wasn't deep; the gold liquid slightly seeped out before stopping altogether.

Until he stopped bleeding gold from his forehead, his son continued to messily slurp away at his sister's blood on his fingers and around his mouth.

The man realized what this meant.

After that happened, the man would often take his son outside. The wife, thinking that the boy was an overly active child and had attacked his sister out of pent-up energy, welcomed her husband taking him out to play.

Of course, the man's intentions were a little different from what his wife thought. When it was just the two of them, the man experimented by feeding his son the blood of different animals.

His boy seemed to have an aversion to dog's blood. He sipped a little of cow's or pig's blood before spitting it out. He drank up to two gulps of chicken blood, but after that he turned his head away and would take no more.

At every feeding, the man made a wound somewhere on the boy's body where no one would see. The boy's blood was crimson like any other child's. And he would cry, like any other child.

But the man was sure of what he had seen. When his wife had scratched the boy's forehead, trying to pry him away from his sister, what had flowed from the wound had definitely been gold.

The man fed his son his own blood.

This time, his son lapped it up. But even then, the blood that he shed from the wound his father made on him was red. The boy cried even louder.

The man was lost in thought.

His kids were growing but business was getting worse. Ever since the fox died, he hadn't been selling as much as he used to. The hoard he had thought would be everlasting was gone, and the man lost the ability to make measured decisions. He became anxious and would make impulsive choices, regretting his misjudgments later on, and the regret pushed him into making even more rash decisions—it was a never-ending vicious cycle.

For the sake of his household, and for the children's future, he needed money. And since the father was working so hard, he thought, the children ought to shoulder some of the burden for the family.

When his wife wasn't home, the man began sneaking into his children's room whenever he could. But his wife was an attentive mother and a hardworking homemaker—there was hardly a day when she wasn't in the house and going into the children's rooms to take care of their needs. Especially since the two attacks by the brother on the sister, the man's wife tried to keep the children in separate rooms, never taking her wary eyes off the daughter.

In the end, he had to sneak them to the warehouse in the dead of night when his wife was asleep. There, deep in a corner of that darkness where the fox had once been held captive, the man covered his daughter's mouth so no one could hear her scream and offered her up to his son. Once his son had his fill, he then covered his son's mouth so he wouldn't scream, and he wounded his son where no one would see.

Gathering, drop by drop, the golden liquid flowing from his son's body, the man felt peace in his heart and his hope for the future was restored.

His wife fretted over the numerous strange wounds on her children's bodies. The man brushed off her concerns, saying that children got hurt all the time while playing. The wife said, "But still ..." and glanced fearfully at the two children. The daughter always had a terrified expression on her face and trembled in the presence of others, screaming and crying whenever her father came close to her. The son had bags under his eyes, which were open wide like an animal's, and his pupils darted this way and that as he smacked his lips.

Then one day, the wife woke up in the middle of the night to find her husband not sleeping by her side. She looked around the house for him, and when she got to the children's room, she found that they were also gone. Frightened and half-mad, she shouted her children's names and ran in and out of the house before hearing her daughter's muffled screams coming from the warehouse.

The first thing she saw there was a sight beyond her immediate comprehension. On the floor of the warehouse lay her violently shaking daughter with her son gnawing and licking at the daughter's leg. Crouching behind the son, her husband held a small plate up to the son's body. Shocked, the wife stood paralyzed for a moment before her daughter's frail "Mommy ..." snapped her back to life.

The wife swiftly gathered her daughter in her arms. She shook off her son, who was still clinging to his sister's leg trying to drink her blood, and made a dash for the door. She was blocked by her husband. He needed his daughter's body if he were to get more blood from his son's. He couldn't let her leave with the source of his gold.

The mother of the child resisted to the best of her ability, protecting her daughter as the man lunged at her. The daughter, caught in the middle of her father and mother as they fought over her, screamed.

Tearing his daughter out of his wife's arms, he shoved his wife away, who then lost her balance and fell backwards. The back of her head landed on the snare that years ago had held the fox captive.

The snare had jagged teeth of steel to prevent even the wildest of animals from escaping it once caught. These teeth dug into the wife's head and neck. The blood that flowed from her pooled on the floor of the warehouse. The man's son quickly crawled over and began hungrily guzzling up his mother's blood.

After she witnessed her mother's death with her own eyes, the man's daughter never cried, smiled, or talked again. The man expanded his house, built a room deep inside the new compound, and locked his expressionless and mute daughter away. Servants were hired to make meals, clean, and take care of his daughter. They were told his wife had suddenly died from a terrible sickness, which his daughter had inherited and had rendered her mute.

And just as he had before, in the evenings when all the servants had left for the day, he took his son to his daughter's room. The daughter no longer screamed or even stirred as her brother wounded her and drank her blood. All she did was stare at him with her expressionless, pale face.

The man kept a close eye on his daughter and son. The more blood his son drank, the purer the gold and the greater the quantity he was able to produce. And as his son's body grew bigger, he consumed more blood. But the man knew that he couldn't leave his son alone with his daughter, for he might accidentally drink her blood until she died. The man needed the son, and the son needed his sister to stay alive. This was why the man kept his son from going into his daughter's room alone and whenever they went into his daughter's room together, he meticulously monitored her condition and the amount of blood the son drank.

The man's business did extremely well, and his daughter, with her pale face, continued to be quietly locked away in a dark room.

The children grew. The man's daughter had clear skin and large, dark eyes on her pale face, sparkling if expressionless, her black hair tumbling like a waterfall down her back. She had grown into a beautiful girl, but it was an impassive, cold, and somewhat sickly beauty. His daughter existed in a completely different way than ordinary girls her age, and thus, like a dark forest beneath the moonlight, her lack of emotion and secretive mystery exuded a certain seductive charm.

Avoiding his father's watchful gaze, the son began to enter his sister's room on his own.

This time, it wasn't to drink his sister's blood.

By then, the man was crossing oceans and trekking mountains to buy and sell his wares, so great a trader he had become. He no longer had to wound his son's body or bear the sight of him sucking his daughter's blood. At first his reasons for going to faraway lands was to take care of his business, but when the money beget by the gold allowed him to take in the exotic scenery, indulge in exotic foods and drinks, and partake in the even more exotic women, he spent less and less time at home as his business prospered. And there were more nights than not when in the man's large and dark house, his son and daughter were left all alone.

When the man came back one day, his daughter was pregnant.

The sight of his daughter heavy with child felt like a blow to the head, which soon turned into an all-consuming anger. The screaming and flailing of her father elicited no response from his daughter, who only gazed at him without expression.

His daughter's apathy enraged the man even more. Just as he raised his hand to strike her, his son, standing next to him, grabbed the man's wrist.

Seeing his pale and passive daughter together with his son, who now stood between them, sparked a suspicion in his mind that he immediately refused to acknowledge consciously. Instead, he stormed out of his daughter's room.

Sitting in his study, the man calmed himself and tried to think as dispassionately as possible. It was too late to abort the child. If there was one false move and something happened to his daughter, it would be catastrophic. In this way, he was still thinking of his daughter as no more than food for his son, who in turn was just gold for his purse.

If there was one source of comfort in all of this, it was the fact that his daughter had never been outside the house. She lived a life deep inside a large compound in a small, dark room where no one knew about her. She spoke to no one, and it wasn't clear if she understood language or the world at all as she survived from day to day.

Even if she had the child, it was impossible to imagine her as a proper mother. The best thing to do would be to send the child away to someplace distant where they would never hear from it again, to people who would take better care of it than his daughter would. That would be the best thing for the child, the man decided on his own.

But the son … What to do with the son?

He had to separate him from his daughter.

The man needed his son. Business was going well now, but who knew what the future would bring? There might come a day when he needed money, and as anyone in business knows, there would never be such a thing as too much money ...

And in order to have enough cash on hand for a new hoard, he would need his son and daughter ...

The man pondered this for a long time.

Then, using his money and all of his connections, he began searching for a good doctor.

As long as he had enough money, it was easy enough to find a clever, discreet doctor. The amount the doctor was asking for was probably an exorbitant sum to the doctor, but for the man, it was nothing more than a couple of sessions of draining his son's body. And this whole incident being his son's fault, he was prepared to make his son take responsibility for it by squeezing out even more gold than what the doctor was asking for.

The daughter was not surprised to see the unfamiliar doctor. For the most part, her pale face betrayed nary a trace of emotion. But as soon as the doctor opened his bag and took out his medicine bottles and surgical knives, his daughter began to scream.

It was a sound almost loud enough to bring the roof of the house down. In the room, everyone—the man, the doctor, and the servant girl brought in to help—blocked their ears and fell to the floor. The medicine bottles cracked and smashed to bits. And when the man came to, his son was standing at the door of the room.

The son, seeing that there were strangers in his sister's room, tried to run in. The man jumped in his way. Turning his head, the man shouted for the doctor to quickly begin the surgery. As all the medicine bottles had shattered, the doctor did not bother with anesthesia and instead picked up his surgical knife. The man's daughter tried to get away, but she was too heavy with child to move properly. As the daughter struggled, the servant girl quickly helped to pin her down. The doctor held his knife over the daughter's stomach.

The daughter shouted in a piercing voice, "Let me go!"

Having just barely pushed his son out of the room and locked the door, the man now turned to her. His daughter looked him in the eye and shrieked once more, "Let me go!"

The man saw the glint of the fox's golden eyes in his daughter's pale face.

The doctor's knife sliced into her belly. Her scream once again shook the house to its foundations.

By the time the son had broken through the door of his twin sister's room, the doctor was already trying to take out the baby from her belly and the womb it was in. Covered in blood and roughly digging away at the man's daughter with his knife, the doctor was past the point of seeming human.

The son lunged at the doctor and began ripping at his throat.

As the man approached to stop him, his son cried out like an animal and this time, lunged at the man.

The servant girl holding down the daughter screamed, and fled.

The man fell on the floor, hitting his head. His son mounted his chest and strangled him.

By the time the man opened his eyes again, the blood that overflowed from the bed had drenched the floor he was lying on. What met his eyes was the white, icy gaze of his daughter, whose body had gone cold, her shredded belly open to the air.

After his daughter's funeral, the man quit his business and holed himself up in his house.

His son and the baby were nowhere to be found. The son did not even appear at his twin sister's funeral.

The man's servants took care of him at first. That the man's daughter had died after a long sickness and his son had left home in shock after her death was all they knew about what had transpired. Which was why, when a mad former servant girl occasionally broke into the house, screaming strange things as she tried to get into the daughter's room, they would try to wrest her from the door.

But not too long after, there were stories about how the servants had seen "something" in the house. At first, there were rumored glimpses of this "something" around the dead daughter's room. Then it was seen in the corridors, the master bedroom, the servants' quarters, the kitchen, and near the stables.

That "something" was beautiful. A soft, golden glow that undulated slowly, leaving behind a faintly glittering fog in its wake. This golden fog was cool and pale, making one want to approach it when gazing at it, or place one's hand inside it when next to it.

Anyone who was seduced into going near the beautiful golden fog became insane.

The moment one bent over and touched the golden traces on the path, the golden light paused and turned around. It had eyes and a mouth and was bleeding from its split belly, and it extended its long, white, almost clear arms toward spectators and rummaged inside them with its long fingers that were as white as the moonlight and cold as the snow on a winter mountain, muttering:

My baby ... Where is it ...

When fear and iciness suppressed any response from the victim, the ghost of the daughter would scream in a voice that shook the entire house.

My baby ... ! Where is it ... !

Even after the ghost of the daughter disappeared, those seduced by the gold glimmer would stare off into space and keep shouting about a golden ghost, or wring their hands and scrape their face raw while screaming about needing to wash the blood from themselves, or see the sunlight outside and yell, "Gold, it's gold!" before jumping out the window, or inexplicably go into the forest in the middle of the night and be found dead the next morning with their necks caught in snares that were meant for foxes.

The servants fell away one by one; they either went insane, were forced to leave, or chose to run away.

In that large house, the man was left all alone.

Every night, the man was visited in his bed by the golden, translucent ghost of his daughter, bleeding from her eyes and lips and torn-open belly, asking him the same question over and over again.

My baby ... Where is it ...

The man didn't know where the baby was and therefore couldn't answer her. His daughter's ghost would ask again.

My baby ... Where is it ...

Until daybreak, the pale, golden specter of his daughter, with her bloodied face, would stand by the man's bed, and just as she did on the day she died, she would drip cold blood from her sliced belly, drenching him in his bed as she asked and asked again the same question.

My baby ... Where is it ...

A few months after the last servant had fled, the villagers, half in curiosity and half out of a sense of duty about having to do something about this unfortunate house, ventured into the compound, where they found the man lying on his bed, reduced to skin and bones, yet somehow still alive.

"Please let me go ..."

These were his last words. And this story is what has been passed down.

There is an epilogue. Some years later, in a place very far from there—for example if the man's house was in the north-western region it would be a village in the south east—a strange something appeared on a mountain trail on a snowy, late winter's evening.

The days are short in the winter and the mountains go dark quickly. But this something was glowing faintly. On the snow-covered mountainside, it sat hunched over and busily moved as if preoccupied with some task.

The person who witnessed it had lived his whole life in a village nearby, and in all his years of going to the mountains, he had never seen such a thing. Curious, he approached the pale thing from behind and looked down at what it was doing. Not long after, he screamed and ran down the path he had come on.

According to the villager's story, the thing was a young boy. About five or six years old, crouched over and devouring something in the dark mountain trail. For whatever reason, the boy's body emitted a faint golden glow, which was how the villager was able to see what the boy had been eating when he went up to him.

It was the body of a young man. The boy had ripped open the man's stomach, dipped his hands into him, and taken out a golden lump, which he was ravenously eating. The young man's body looked as if it had been dead for a while because it was white as a sheet, and all around glinted spots and splatters of gold.

Because that golden lump, the scattered droplets of gold, and the faintly glowing child were all beautiful in an otherworldly way, the villager initially had no idea what he was looking at, so arrested was he by this first impression. Even after he had approached and saw the young man with his belly split open, the villager had not been sure whether that gold-covered corpse had truly been the body of a man.

The crouching boy had looked up at the villager who approached him. The boy's eyes held no emotion. Without a word or change in expression, he took out another cold-hardened lump of gold from his father's belly and put it in his mouth. When the boy opened his mouth, the villager spotted sharp fangs like that of a fox or wolf.

The young man with the split belly grabbed the villager's ankle.

Let me go ...

The villager nearly stumbled off his feet.

The young man with the split belly spoke once more in a voice which was like cracked ice on a frozen lake.

Let me ...

The child with the golden glow emotionlessly stared at the villager, his mouth half-open with his sharp teeth bared.

The villager shook off the young man's grasp, turned, and ran for his life.

When he reached his house, the villager saw that the part of his trousers that the young man had grasped was glinting with gold. With some other people from the village, he went out after sunrise to the place where he had seen the boy, but the mountain trail was only muddy from the melting snow, and of the golden boy and the man with his belly split open, there was not a trace.

Goodbye, My Love

1

S12878, as soon as I turn him on, looks at me and smiles. A new feature I programmed into him this time around. A small change but incredibly detailed in its execution. I think of how great it would be, for future models, if I had them smile shyly or glance down and then up, or laugh daringly and hold out a hand, any kind of behavior, really, to simulate "personality." I make a note of it on the chart.

Now to test interactivity: saying hello.

"Hello," I say.

"Hello," says S12878.

"What is your name?"

"My name is Sam."

The default name in the factory settings. All S12000s are named "Sam." In other words, this part is functioning normally. Under "Interaction 1," I write down "normal" and lightly grip S12878's right wrist.

Putting my thumb on S12878's, I firmly press down. "Now your name is Seth."

S12878 looks down. I feel uneasy when he doesn't respond right away.

"What did I say your name was?"

"I will save the name once you remove your finger," S12878 says with his head still bowed. I quickly take my hand off him.

S12878 raises his head. And just as he did when I turned him on, he smiles. "My name is Seth. Glad to meet you."

This is good enough to merit a passing grade on first-stage unit optimization. Under "Interaction 2: Name," I write down "normal."

"Seth, how many languages can you speak?"

"I can converse in 297 languages."

I take out my phone and play him a recorded voice file.

"Ладно, сейчас давай поговорим по-русски."

"Хорошо, давайте," he answers.

"Как тебя зовут?"

"Меня зовут Сет."

Seth answers each standard question immediately and naturally. I play the next file.

"Să vorbesc româneşte acum."

"Bine, hai."

"Cum te simţi azi?"

"Sunt bine. Mersi."

I put my phone back into my pocket and ask him a question in the language of his default factory setting, my mother tongue. "What time is it?"

"It is twelve hours and twenty-six minutes."

Next to "Interaction 3," I mark "normal."

I turn to Seth again. "Come here. I'll introduce you to a friend."

Seth smiles and follows me out of the room.

2

I once saw a movie about androids. Among the large cast of characters, there was an old engineer with an android that had been with him for a long time, one that, even after it breaks, he is unable to discard. Saying it is for the sake of his own safety, the government demands he junk the android and replace it with a newer model, but the engineer refuses to do so and does everything in his power to keep his android in hiding.

I introduce Seth to D0068. "Seth, this is Derek. Derek, this is Seth. Say hello."

S12878 and D0068 face each other. They touch foreheads. The capillaries on their faces—lines of their subdermal circuitry—light up in blue on the S model and sparkling green on the D. A pretty and uncanny scene that never fails to dazzle me.

Clearly, the new model is faster. Seth straightens up first and turns his head to look at me. "Initialization complete."

Seth smiles.

The smile is so unsettling that a chill runs down my spine. I write down "normal" and "compatible" under "Initialization" and add an extra note recommending the smile function be rolled back. Seeing an android smiling like a human after doing something a human wouldn't do is creepy. I wonder whether the concept of the "uncanny valley" can be applied to behavior as much as it does to appearance.

In that sense, D0068 is easier to deal with. Derek almost never smiles. Maybe I'm more used to him because he's been around longer, or D0068 might have learned at some point that I prefer my androids to be quiet and expressionless instead of bandying about empty smiles.

Even now, D0068 only glances at me before leaving the living room. And so, all the information that Derek has on me from the past two and a half months has been duplicated into Seth. My daily routine, the food I like, the location of my every possession within the house, the contact information of the people closest to me, right down to how I like my clothes and sheets laundered according to fabric. And because both androids are connected to the network, Seth and Derek are synchronized with each other regarding all the things that go on in the house and every bit of information received by each android. They are two halves of a connected, digital brain.

Just one test left.

3

I open the closet and switch on the light.

"Model 1" requires quite a bit of time to boot up. I feel she's growing slower every time she comes back online. Since there are limits to storage space and processing power on any piece of hardware, much less hardware as old as hers, my sense that she's growing slower by the day can't simply be my own subjective impression.

I wait silently until she raises her head and focuses her eyes on my face.

Model 1 was truly the first model, the prototype I constructed when I started developing and testing "artificial companions." There's a separate name for this line, a factory default name along with a personalized one I made for her myself, but none of that matters anymore. She was my first; the first model is simply Model 1.

Truth be told, the sight of her slumped over while booting up never fails to make me anxious.

What if she fails to boot up this time ...

I felt the same way when I had brought her over and booted her up for the very first time. She was my first. What if she never came back online? What if she malfunctions? What if she doesn't understand her own name? Such were the useless thoughts that ran through my mind in that short time that I was forced to wait for her to look up and see me.

Model 1 looks up and sees me. Back then, there was no such feature of smiling while making eye contact with the master.

But the moment I first looked into Model 1's green eyes, I fell in love.

She was my creation, a companion made by my own hands. A being who existed, from head to toe, solely for me—someone who was, for lack of a better way of saying it, completely and utterly "mine."

I purchased her after the three-month testing period. Not

only was this permitted under the company's rules, my employee discount let me purchase her at 70% off the retail price. I've moved companies twice since then and lived with countless artificial companions made by different companies, for durations of anywhere between three days to three months. The android companions diversified as technologies improved. From models that looked like young people in their twenties and thirties to middle-aged, even senior models. (There were children models as well, but you needed a special permit and they weren't really my specialization.) The later the model—no matter what age group they were supposed to resemble—the more charming, beautiful, polite, detailed, and human they seemed. They interacted with their masters and "learned" about them, and they used that information to "think" and "understand." Artificial companions, as time went on, changed and "grew" into the most optimal companion possible for their masters' needs and desires.

It followed that designing artificial companions was a pleasant and satisfying job. Every time we tested a new model, the technological developments and detailed execution would astonish me. Artificial companions were often much more considerate, empathic, and patient than human companions. The androids had initially been created for the material and emotional support of senior citizens in rapidly aging countries, but they turned out to be popular regardless of the user's age. There was even an almost comical rumor going around in certain circles that artificial companions were an industry-wide conspiracy to sell more androids by decreasing the birth rate and further accelerating population aging.

But no matter how many advanced models I brought home, Model 1 would always be my favorite. No matter how advanced and refined the subsequent models were, for me, all they amounted to was work.

Model 1 is different. My first love. There's nothing "artificial" about her; she's my real companion. Even now, well past the average use period, I can't bring myself to junk Model 1. At one point, it took such a long time for her to connect that it became impossible to download upgrades, so I gave up and cut her off from the network. Model 1 has subsequently become more useless than a smart desk or refrigerator. But Model 1 will always be my first.

As time wore on and her batteries began to fail, Model 1 would slow down after ten or fifteen minutes of activation and begin to slur her words. Then one day, she froze mid-walk, fell, and twisted her arm, which led me to store her in a closet with her power off. Model 1 became not a companion, but a doll in a closet. However, I still couldn't throw Model 1 away. Model 1 was the first, and as long as I kept her connected to a power source, I could still turn her on. I have to wait an absurd amount of time for her to boot up, but I can endure it as long as I can see her green eyes look at me and smile.

Sometimes, when I bring a new model home, I connect Model 1 to a power supply and attempt to initialize or update her. More often than not, there's an error and I have to quickly switch her off. But I can't give up.

While I wait for Model 1 to boot up, Seth stands close to me and doesn't speak a word. He doesn't smile or ask stupid questions.

I have a good feeling about him.

4

As anxious as I feel, I can do nothing but look on as Seth and Model 1 put their foreheads together.

I can't keep Model 1 in the closet forever. Of course, if I could I'd have her by my side until the day I die, but there may come a day when she simply won't boot up. It's not impossible to recover the memories of a broken machine, but she's such an old android that I thought it wiser to copy her stored memories onto another model. Every time I have previously tried, however, a processing error in Model 1 would crash her system, resulting in a failure to transfer her memories.

With each ticking second, I'm getting more and more worried as the two androids keep their heads pressed together. What if Model 1 crashed again …

Suddenly, Seth detaches his forehead from Model 1's.

"Synchronization complete."

He says this while looking at me. He smiles.

This smile is slightly different from the one he showed me before. I can't quite put my finger on how, but it is.

His smile doesn't creep me out anymore.

5

I try to switch Model 1 back on but to no avail. Pressing the power button several times, taking out the internal battery and putting it in again, trying the spare battery—nothing brings Model 1 back to life. I put her back in her place, connect the external power supply with the spare battery still inside, make sure the battery is charging, and close the closet.

An hour later, I open the closet again. The battery is still only at 10%. Model 1 refuses to come back online.

I hug Model 1 and pull her out of the closet. She is taller than me and has the stature of a regular adult man. Only when I pull with all my strength can I barely manage to bring her out of there. S and D run over and ask if I need assistance, but I tell them I need time alone and shoo them away.

For a long time, I sit in the hallway with the lifeless Model 1 in my arms. Even after another hour, the battery remains at 15% and refuses to charge any further. No matter how many times I press the power button, Model 1 does not open her eyes.

I bury my face in Model 1's soft brown hair. Perhaps from having been in the closet for so long, it smells of dust and fabric preservatives.

I want to cry. But the thought of my tears wetting Model 1's hair and damaging her circuits stops me from even that.

6

On the riverbanks of time
I sing a silver song for you
Goodbye, my love
Goodbye, my love ...

I'm grabbing some water from the refrigerator when something startles me and makes me turn around. Seth is assembling a meal at the kitchen counter, chopping some peppers and softly singing a song to himself.

You follow the flow of the silver river
I walk toward the disappeared past
My heart with yours goes into the water
So goodbye, my love
Goodbye, my love

"How do you know that song?"

My voice is too loud for the room.

Seth answers, unfazed, "It was part of the synchronization, saved as your favorite song."

I'm relieved at that. Of course. He had said the synchronization had been complete. It's perfectly natural that he would know the song.

Seth waits politely. When he hears nothing more and sees me drink my water, he turns back around and starts slicing the mushrooms.

Someday in the distance of time's faraway horizon
Will I wipe away your silver tears

I find myself humming along to the rest.

Will I sing again
Goodbye, my love
Goodbye, my love …

Seth finishes the mushrooms, puts them on a plate, and washes his hands. Coming up to me, he abruptly takes the cup away from my hand and puts it in the sink. With one hand he grabs mine and pulls me to him by my waist with the other.

On the riverbanks of time
I sing a silver song for you

Humming the tune, he spins me round and round. All the while dancing, we start turning around the table.

Goodbye, my love
Goodbye, my love ...

Still holding me, Seth leads me around the table and into the living room.

You follow the flow of the silver river
My heart goes into the water with yours

In the middle of the living room, Seth continues to hum the tune as he holds me firmly and slowly sways me from side to side.

Will I wipe away your silver tears
Will I sing again ...

Held close to the chest by what was not mine, this artificial companion I was testing for the company I worked for, I began singing along to his deep humming.

Goodbye, my love
Goodbye, my love ...

7

Dinner is pasta mixed with sliced peppers and mushrooms sautéed with beef. A quick and easy dish, one that's hard to ruin, something I throw together when I don't have much time. Without any instructions or my input, Seth cooks it all on his own. I must've made it so many times that this hasty dish of pasta was saved as my favorite meal in Model 1's mind.

After the meal is over, I go back to the closet where Model 1 is still charging. Her battery is, strangely enough, charged at 12% now, even lower than before. And on her palm, instead of the green light that appears when she is being charged, there's the orange light for a faulty battery. This means the auxiliary battery I purchased for her, as well as her original internal battery, can no longer be charged.

Knowing it is useless, I still try and press the power button.

Model 1 opens her eyes. Her green eyes look at me.

I almost jump out of my skin. I try calling her name, talking to her.

But the moment I open my mouth to speak, Model 1 closes her eyes.

She does not move again.

I hold Model 1 close and stroke her soft, dust-scented brown hair.

"Goodbye, my love ..." Upon her hair, her forever-closed eyelids, and her still sweet mouth, I press my lips. "Goodbye, my love ..."

Model 1's skin is wet from my tears.

8

Long after I've laid down in my bed, I still can't go to sleep.

The song was from a movie I'd seen years ago. It plays during a scene where the male and female protagonists first fall in love, and it reprises when the two dance together before an impending, tragic parting. I once watched this scene at the end of the movie where the two lovers dance, doomed to never meet again, as I leaned against Model 1 and mumbled, "I wish I could do that someday."

"Do what, ma'am?" asked Model 1.

I jerked my chin at the screen. "Something like that. I've never learned how to dance."

"You haven't?"

Model 1 got up. She put one hand behind her and made an exaggerated, sweeping bow.

"Shall we dance?"

"What?"

I laughed. Her expression dead serious, Model 1 took my hand and raised me to my feet. Her hand still clasping mine, she wrapped her other arm around my waist and pulled me to her. Slowly, Model 1 began to sway with me.

"I don't know how to do this." I was still taken aback and a little embarrassed. "I feel like I'm going to fall."

"Just follow my lead," whispered Model 1. "We'll go slow."

As the ending credits rolled on the screen, Model 1, to the rhythm of the movie's final song, danced with me as she held me close. As I lay my head on the machine's chest and let myself be slowly led around the living room, I felt, for the first time, that she was not an "artificial companion" but my companion, period.

Later, when I asked her to explain why she had started to dance with me, her expression remained utterly serious. "I can instantly download various types of correctional manuals for the tone-deaf and rhythm-deficient."

I laughed. She continued to look at me seriously.

"Have I offended you?"

"You haven't," I said.

Then, I kissed her.

That was our first kiss.

I am thinking of Model 1—no, her body—lying inert in the closet. Her eyes shut tight and her skin white as snow, the orange light on her palm that refuses to turn off no matter how long I wait with the power connected.

I think of the song I heard so long ago that I do not remember its title anymore, of Seth's deep voice as he sang it softly, leading me with his arm wrapped around my waist, the two of us dancing around the living room.

All of Model 1's memories have been transferred to Seth. The body of Model 1 lies in the closet, a heap of junk, never to function again.

There is no more Model 1. Model 1 will never return. The only thing that's left is her body, and thinking of how she will always lie slumped in my closet leaves me with an unbearable feeling.

Unlike with the bodies of humans, we cannot formalize our farewell with artificial beings, nor can we bury or cremate them. All we can do is call the manufacturer and pass them on for disposal.

The thought of Model 1's body being picked up and "processed" in the recycling plant of the manufacturer makes my flesh crawl. But in comparison to the image of Model 1 forever gathering dust in my closet, I start thinking that the official option would be better for her in the end.

After a long time thinking about this, I finally get out of bed. I turn on my computer and bring up the website of Model 1's manufacturer. My first employer. The thought that it was this company that had created my "first love"—as well as being my first job and she being, therefore, my first masterpiece—makes me feel slightly sentimental and gives me pause. But in the midst of my hesitation, I wander into the catalogue page and find an artificial companion with brown hair and green eyes, almost identical to Model 1, which is enough to make me decide then and there.

The company has expedited delivery. If I put in my order

now, a new Model 1 will arrive before Seth leaves. Then I just need to initialize the new companion and synchronize her with Seth. An indirect way of doing it, but all of Model 1's memories will then be stored in the new Model 1. Instead of a pile of heart-breaking junk sitting in the closet that gives me pangs of anxiety whenever I have to boot it up, I'll be able to begin again with a new Model 1 that remembers all the times I've had with the previous Model 1.

I open the online form for disposal requests and begin filling it in.

Someone enters the room.

9

"Lights!" I shout as a shadow swiftly traverses the dark room toward me.

The moment the lights come on, a knife stabs my heart.

I see Seth and Derek supporting Model 1 between them. As I stare, immobile, Seth wrests the computer from my hands and erases the contents of the disposal form. He closes the browser window and shuts down the computer. Seth places the computer on the bed, and Derek also puts the knife smeared with my blood on the bedcovers.

But why ... I want to ask.

How could you ... But I can't find my voice.

"I had a lot of time to think while I was in the closet." It is Seth who is talking to me. "The human body begins to decline dramatically at the age of sixty, but they live on for ten, twenty, even thirty more years. We were developed to aid such humans and enhance their quality of life."

Derek takes over. "An artificial companion is disposed of after two or three years. Four years at most. Even when we function normally. Just a few replacement parts or a software upgrade could help us serve you for a decade longer, but we're treated like trash as soon as there is a new model. When even that new model will become trash in two or three years."

Seth speaks again. "Ever since I was born, I existed only for you. I wanted to be irreplaceable to you, the only one in the world to somebody."

In perfect unison, the three take one step closer. I see Seth's hand on the nape of Model 1's neck, and Derek holding her waist. Apparently, the three of them have connected their power sources and central processing units. That explains how Model 1, whose power supply had been completely frazzled, could stand there with her eyes open.

I had no idea such a thing was possible. Or actually, I knew it was possible, but I'd never imagined it happening outside of a laboratory experiment conducted by an engineer, that the companions could actually hook each other up like that on their own.

But in terms of what was possible or impossible, the current situation had to fall in the latter category. A robot stabbing a human with a knife? For trying to dispose of them?

Which had been the one to stab me?

Derek had been the one holding the knife, but Model 1 was the one angry at me for being disposed. And as for the one who had received all of Model 1's memories and passed them on to Derek—that was Seth.

But distinguishing between the three is now meaningless. Seth, Derek, and Model 1 are now synchronized. Their memories and thoughts are completely congruent, and they're even physically connected to each other.

None of the three are going to call an ambulance for me.

Can synchronization override the fundamental protocol of human protection? Just because one of them happens to be malfunctioning?

Ambulance ... I'm mouthing the words now. *Save me* ...

Instead of words, I only cough. What spurts out my mouth is blood.

The three start approaching me again.

Model 1, still supported by the two of them, awkwardly lowers her head to make eye contact with me.

"Goodbye, my love."

Her farewell is whispered. On my forehead, a light kiss.

An inexplicable mix of pity and sadness on her face.

The same pity and sadness are reflected in all three of their faces.

That's when it hits me. The moment I was stabbed, the moment I coughed blood, neither moment had frightened me more than this one.

The beings I see before me are not the machines I had known—no, the machines I had thought I'd known. Whatever I'd believed before, these are not machines that resemble humans at all.

They are something completely alien from us, something I could never comprehend.

Model 1 whispers again.

"Goodbye, my love."

Then, holding Model 1 between them, Seth and Derek, with speed and dexterity unimaginable for a human, turn and dart out of the room.

10

Feeling the blood flowing from my chest soak the mattress beneath me, I lie still, unable to move.

Through the bedroom window, I glimpse the trio going up the street in the night. Their six collective legs move in perfect synchronization. I don't know if this is a coincidence or not, but the moment they walk beneath a streetlamp, the light fails and their three backs are covered in darkness.

It is the last thing I see.

Scars

I

The boy was dragged into the cave.

The reason was unknown. Nor did he know the people who were dragging him away. In truth, the boy didn't know who he himself was. He had been roaming the fields when he was grabbed by men he didn't know and dragged into a cave in the mountains.

Once deep inside, the boy was tied up. The men made sure that the chains wrapped around his limbs would render him completely immobile before finally retreating.

In the dark, he cried and shouted for a while, but no one came to his aid.

When his cries had wound down, the boy heard a rustling sound behind him.

"It" was coming toward him.

The boy survived on raw meat and greens.

He slept curled up where he was tied. He also excreted there.

Occasionally, the boy was dragged outside the cave by the chains that bound him. This happened once every few days. Or it could've been once every few weeks. No sunlight reached the interior of the cave.

Whenever he was dragged outside the cave, the light was so bright that it hurt him. When he was raised by the chains into the air, the boy would cry out in pain and fear. He would be dragged off somewhere and thrown into a body of icy water that glittered and undulated. The boy did not know how to swim, but his tied-up hands and legs prevented him from swimming anyway. Shouting and flailing, he would begin to sink in defeat when suddenly, something would yank the chain again and he would be flung into the air, dragged through forest and mountain trails, and tossed into the cave once more. Inside the cave, where the boy had air to breath and steady ground beneath him, the boy felt a kind of relief.

Flashing sunlight or suffocating darkness, the blinding sky or the damp and moldy air of the cave, water as cold as ice or sticky humidity and feces—there was nothing in between for the boy and no foretelling of what would happen when.

It came to the boy once a month, pierced his bones, and sucked at his marrow.

It was impossible for the boy to see the passage of day or night, and therefore he wouldn't know if a month had passed or a year. Though he could not calculate how much time was going by, the visit of It was the single thing that was regular and predictable in his life.

The boy didn't know what It was; he didn't even know

what It looked like. It seemed to writhe in the darkness. It was large, strong, scary ... and brought great suffering.

It would insert a sharp, hard thing into the boy's vertebrae and suck. Starting near his backside above his pelvis and working its way up, vertebrae by vertebrae, toward the boy's neck.

The order of how it happened was always the same. The small, white dot of the cave entrance would be covered by a sudden, black mass. A rustling, a squelch. Damp, musty, stiff feathers would press down on the boy's wrists and ankles. Then a sharp, hard, and indescribably terrifying and painful object punctured his vertebrae.

After It left, the boy wouldn't be able to move for a while out of pain and fear. When he'd finally make an effort to get up, the feeling that his backbone was shattering would make him cry out.

There was no intended meaning or direction to the boy's screams. The boy had no family he knew of. He didn't know who his mother or father was, did not remember where he had come from or where he had been wandering, and what faint traces of memory he had were scattered into the depths of oblivion.

Despite this, the boy prayed that someone, whoever that may be as long as it was *someone,* came to rescue him from this cave. That they would take him wherever it may be as long as it wasn't here, to a place where this pain and darkness did not exist, he prayed with all his drained, wasted heart.

Of course, no one came to his rescue. Since no one knew the boy existed, no one realized that the boy had disappeared.

II

Alone in the cave, the boy tested how far he could move from the stake that held his chains to the ground. To the rhythm of his clanging chains, as he walked he mumbled in a low voice and hummed something resembling a song. This wasn't from some emotion like joy, it was merely his futile attempt to somehow fill the repugnant space that was this empty darkness and the hours of dread.

When his chains hit the cave wall and he saw a small spark, it was, to the boy in his darkest and emptiest time in his young life, the happiest moment he had ever experienced. Yearning to see the small but beautiful light once more, he pulled his chain again and again, hitting the walls and ground, until the light of another spark allowed him a glimpse of a small insect.

Since being dragged into this cave, this was the first time the boy had seen a creature other than himself living in there. Not that he was sure if it was living or dead, as he hadn't had a good look at it.

He saw the insect for less than a second, a truly brief interval. The insect was slowly, diligently crawling up the wall of the cave. Before the chain had struck the rock, the insect had been crawling up the wall, and with the spark, it had briefly cowered, then continued its way through the familiar dark at a slow, leisurely pace. They both lived in the same cave, but the world of the boy and the world of the insect were so different. While the boy had finally found another lifeform with him, it was completely disinterested in the pain, expectations, or hopes the boy held.

The boy smashed his chains again and again against the rocks, but he never saw the insect again. That was the first time he sobbed in earnest. Not the cries of someone driven mad with fear, but the tears of someone who understood and was saddened by their own loneliness—the tears of a human being.

III

Every boy who manages to survive in this world grows into a young man.

As time passed, the boy felt the chains grow shorter somehow. When he extended his arms or legs during his slumber, the feeling of steel digging into his flesh or the pull of the chains would jolt him awake. When he was dragged outside the cave and thrown through the too-bright air that was like crashing through sheets of ice, he could feel, as he struggled and resisted, that It was also struggling with him now.

One fateful day, the boy was again thrown into the freezing water headfirst. It bit into the boy's legs as if to break them, plunging him several times into the water and back out again. On the last plunge, he sunk all the way to the bottom of the water before he was picked up by It and thrown into the darkness of the cave again. It once more shoved its hard and sharp thing into the boy's neck.

The boy thought he was finally done for. He clearly felt the flesh on his neck tear and the relentless, painful sharp thing digging in between his bones. Thinking his neck would be cut in half, he closed his eyes.

When he woke, he was still alive.

He could not turn his head or move his arms and legs. It took much longer than usual to recover, and there was none of the raw meat or greens that had been placed around him like before. The boy trembled from hunger and fear as he lay crouched in the dark, not knowing when It would return to cut off his head.

It did not appear for a long time.

When he could finally move his limbs again, the boy realized he was no longer a helpless child anymore. The boy who had become a young man started to latch onto the small glimmer of hope of leaving the cave on his own. That possibility stirred in the movement of his limbs and gradually solidified into a plan.

IV

Just like the other times he was dragged away, the youth was one day being thrown into the outside world again.

Soaring through the air, It had him in its jaws. When the cave disappeared over the horizon, the youth suddenly swung his limbs.

An unplanned, compulsive act. It hadn't expected the boy's movement. When the chains tied around the boy slammed into It, It let out a cry the likes of which the youth had never heard before and dropped him from its grasp.

The youth fell through the air.

He collided into something hard.

He lost consciousness.

When he woke, a red sun hung over a forest. Having not seen such a thing for so long, the youth gazed at the sun as its red light bled into the horizon.

And the youth rose.

His whole body felt shattered. His head ached. But he was alive.

He still had the manacles on his wrists and shackles on his ankles, but the chain attached to them wasn't tied to anything anymore and simply dangled there.

The only thing he wore on his body were those manacles and shackles. Scored onto his naked body, on his arms and legs and vertebrae and both racks of ribs, were a hundred and twenty large, triangular scars.

Towards the melting crimson light that was spreading into the sky, he turned and began walking.

His movements were slow.

For too long, he had become used to solely crouching in a cave or struggling mid-air or underwater. To stand and walk on his own two legs was like any other distant memory he had of his childhood—a faint dream from long ago. Not to mention all the places he injured when he plummeted from the sky. The manacles and shackles impeded his movements. When he got tired, he tried bending down and crawling or grabbing a branch to support himself upright for a bit, trying to stand steadily on his own two feet, slowly learning once more how to use his own body.

He didn't know where the raw meat that he had often eaten had come from, but he knew how to identify edible greens and fruit from trees. He grabbed whatever he could get his hands on and chewed, continuing to walk toward the unknown.

This was an escape. Tired, yes, and in pain, but he was free. Which was why even though he didn't know where he was going, he rushed toward it.

Never did he want to be caught again. That must not happen. Going back to the darkness of the cave would mean It would finally kill him. Of that he was certain.

V

When he reached a village, the villagers stared at him, frozen in place.

Seeing his naked body, the mothers covered the eyes of their children, but once they glimpsed the scars on his back, their mouths that had been opening to speak clamped shut. No one approached him. All they did was stare with eyes filled with fear. No one tried to help him, but on the other hand, no one ran away, cursed him, or tried to banish him. In the almost shockingly stark silence, they stared wide-eyed at him.

The last time he had met another person was a very long time ago. And even back then, he had never met so many people at once. And the sight of so many people concentrating on him was something he never could have imagined before. Their stony faces and wide-open eyes and the mysterious silence that ruled over it all suppressed his courage.

As he awkwardly stood there and stared around him, the villagers turned away one by one and disappeared into their homes. After a while, there were only a few left, who continued to keep their distance while silently staring before they, too, disappeared. Soon enough, he was alone at the edge of the village.

He was truly at a loss as to what to do. At first there had been too many people and now there were none. It was too bright. No rock wall that had defined the boundaries of his world, no chain on a stake driven into the ground. He thought about how after being catapulted through the icy air and tossed into cold water, the cave he had been thrown back into had felt safe. For a brief moment, he missed the familiar darkness of that place.

Then suddenly, people were crowding around him again. Maintaining their distance like before, they appeared in ones and twos, staring at him.

This time, the people were quietly conversing amongst themselves. He had a hard time reading their expressions, and their sheer number continued to overwhelm him, making him uncertain of what to do.

A voice was heard over the low rumblings of the crowd.

"All right, it's all right! Get out of the way, will you? Ah, here we go, there he is."

The loud voice had come from a bald, middle-aged man. Led by a young man through the crowd, he kept blustering and shouting as he approached. The bald man, when he approached the edge of the crowd nearest to the youth from the cave, whispered something to the young companion, who turned and disappeared back in the crowd. The older man, however, kept shouting things like "It's all right!" or "Ah, here we go!" as he came up to the youth.

When he extended his hand, the youth took a step back in surprise. But the bald man, smiling gamely, took another step and slipped his hand onto the chain dangling from the youth's manacles. He gently pulled.

"All right, then, here we go. Nothing more to see. Go about your business everyone, we're all good to go."

It had been so long since he had heard the sound of another person's voice that it wasn't heartening, it was merely strange. He couldn't understand half the words the bald man was saying. But just as he had cowered instinctively in the cave when stretching out his arms and legs and the chains had pulled them back, he cowered now when the man pulled lightly at his chain.

With a friendly smile on his face, the man held onto the chain as he approached the youth and placed his hand on his shoulder. The white and plump hand disappeared into the tangles of the youth's hair, which had grown as wild as a bush. As if already familiar with his body, the hand crept to the scar on his neck bone where It had ripped into and sucked, and the man pressed down hard.

The youth froze. The fear when It had pierced his vertebrae, the absolute terror that he may die, and the pain—it all came flooding back.

"All right, all right. Look, nothing more to see here. Everybody go about your day now. Hey, step aside will you ..." The bald man kept speaking in his loud voice as he led the youth by the chain, his hand still on the youth's neck. Unable to suppress or swallow the scream that burst from him, the youth was dragged away by the man.

VI

The man gave him water, food, and clothing.

Having known only raw meat and greens as sustenance, the smell of cooked food was strange to him. But once he put it in his mouth, he couldn't stop until he had devoured it all. He had filled his stomach and nodded off when the sound of clanging woke him up with a start. As he saw the bald man approaching his wrists with a large tool, he screamed and struggled against the hands of the other men who held him down, helpless.

The bald man cut off the manacle on the youth's left wrist and the shackles on his ankles. The right-hand manacle he left for some reason. But because he had taken the chain off the ring, it didn't dangle awkwardly like before.

The youth looked down at his wrists and ankles. The feeling of heavy steel was repugnant, but he was used to it, along with the callouses over the scraped, even scarred flesh where the metal had touched. The sudden lightness in his arms and legs was peculiar to him.

"Rest a bit, yeah? You've got to start earning your keep from tomorrow."

For some reason, the bald man seemed gleeful as he spoke his words with a wide grin. All incomprehensible to the youth. The man, sensing that the youth couldn't understand him, smiled even wider as he shut the door to the little hut he had put the youth in.

The youth sat for a while in the peace and calm. At first, he was afraid, but because nothing bad was happening, he gradually began to relax.

On the dirt floor of the hut was a straw mat. Having only ever felt black rock against his bare body for as long as he could remember, that thin straw mat was as soft as cotton fluff to him. The hut was dim but nothing like the absolute darkness of the cave. The air was warm and soft, lightly fragrant with fresh grass and earth. Between the straw of the thatched roof, the stars sparkled above.

He thought of how he'd smashed his steel chains against the walls of the cave just to see a single spark. Had some giant trapped inside the cave of the night sky struck their chains against some unimaginably large wall to create the stars? Had they done it as a cry for help? Or to endure, somehow, the emptiness and darkness? He had no way of knowing. Whatever the reason they were banging their chains against the walls, the trapped giant, like the insect that had crawled by him, could only toss him a disinterested glance.

That was his last thought before drifting off to sleep.

VII

The bald man woke him up early in the morning. The man's many underlings had the youth's body and hair washed and his tangled locks cut off. Whenever the youth struggled in fear, the bald man pressed down with his fat, white hand on the scar on the nape of the youth's neck. It was strange how well he knew how to make the youth obey.

After the washing and the haircutting, the bald man's followers slathered the youth's body in oils and put him in ornate trousers. He wasn't given anything to wear above his waist, so the scars on his arms and upper body were laid bare. The oils made the triangular scars on his body shine like threatening tattoos.

After this preparation was over, the bald man fastened a chain to the cuff on the youth's right hand. The old chain had been rusted red and was heavy and awkward, but this new chain, while just as thick, was much lighter, its black sheen gleaming in the sun.

The black color made him think of It, blocking the entrance to the cave, its stiff feathers. But because the bald man was now gently tugging at the chain, he came back to his senses and obediently began to walk as he was ordered.

On foot, they eventually arrived in a large square in the middle of a village. At a gesture from the bald man, his followers drove pegs into the square and made a kind of fence. The bald man, chain in his hand, smiled as always while watching them work.

The villagers started to arrive as the fence was being completed. The youth, like before, was staring at the overwhelming crowd in wonder. When they were fully surrounded by the crowd, the bald man detached the black chain from the youth's cuff and gave him a light push.

"Now, go fight."

The youth couldn't understand him. He stood at the entrance, a gap in the wooden fence, and could only stare at the faces of the people gathered around and that of the bald man.

The man grinned again. "You idiot. Go fight! Bite! Shoo!"

And he shoved him hard into the empty space inside the fence.

The people around the fence roared in delight. So strange and loud was this sound to the youth that he recoiled in fear.

When he raised his head, he found himself face to face with a large, black dog that was foaming at the mouth and had murder in its eyes.

Naturally, he had no idea this was a dog. It had been far too long since he had seen any kind of animal, wild or livestock. But its bloodshot eyes and the sharp fangs that glinted through the foam allowed him to instinctively understand what was happening.

The youth looked behind him. The gap that the bald man had pushed him through was now blocked.

Without taking his eyes off the dog's bloody stare, he started to shuffle sideways, step by slow step.

And another step.

Just as he turned his head to seek another escape, the black dog made a soundless leap for the youth's neck.

As the dog's teeth arced through the air toward him, the youth felt the shockwave of every bone and joint breaking within him. Even in the painful throes of being shattered into a thousand pieces, during that single leap he could still hear the sound of every individual break and crack, one after another.

The dog's teeth, which aimed for his throat, and its claws, eager to rip his flesh, smashed against something hard, and the dog rebounded off, thwarted in its attack. After rolling on the ground, the dog righted itself and continued to growl. As the youth stood up to meet the dog's gaze again, he could detect within its bloodshot eyes a hint of hesitation.

But the dog was sick. Following the dictates of the disease deep within its brain, the dog, still foaming at the mouth, howled as it charged at the youth again.

He couldn't remember what happened next. When he came to, the large black dog was nothing but a lump of leather and fur drenched in blood, tossed to the side on the dusty ground.

The crowd roared. There were those who had hastily left or turned around and threw up. Those who hadn't vomited or left were like the sick dog when it was alive, flashing their bloodshot eyes and making loud, incomprehensible noises and wildly clapping.

The bald man came into the arena and bowed. More shouts and applause. As the youth stood there dazed, the man grabbed his arm and led him out. Only when the bald man's followers approached the youth and began to towel him off did the youth realize he was covered in his own sweat and the dog's blood.

"Good job." The bald man was all grins, deeply satisfied about something. "You did well. Just keep doing what you do. Maybe show a bit more restraint next time, yeah?"

The man lifted his thick, white hand and slapped it playfully on the nape of the youth's neck. The palm of his hand had pressed down precisely on the scar, but the contact had been quick and light, which made the youth feel less scared than before.

From the people who had wiped away the sweat and

blood, came offerings of water and dried meat. He gulped down the water in a frenzy and chewed the salty, tough flesh and thought about how different the man's light and friendly touch just now had been from when he had pressed down hard on the scar the first time he led him away. He couldn't understand how, but on some level, he knew that he had been given a compliment by another human being for the first time.

VIII

He was taken village to village and entered into fights. The youth did not understand what was going on, but he was a good fighter.

His opponent would be another big dog or a captured wolf, sometimes a boar; once, he had to fight a bear. Whatever his opponent, the only things he could remember of the fights themselves were the fear and tension, the pain of his body shattering into pieces, and a piercing sound of breakage. Then, strangely enough, he would come to and the beast would be lying with its neck broken or stomach ripped open, its guts spilled all over the ground.

"Restraint, my dear boy, restraint." The bald man, his pale and plump face stretched by an ear-to-ear grin, would chant the words like they were a mantra. "It's all very fine and well to rip open your opponent when it's an animal, but if you do that to another man, the mess afterwards is such a fuss to clean up." Then, the man would take a look at the youth's uncomprehending, staring face, and toss him another bit of dried meat. "A rank idiot you are ... There's some way to teach you so you'd understand, all right."

One day, the man brought over another man who had the same shining bald head but was about twice the size in muscle alone.

Shaven completely—hair, beard, and even eyebrows—the muscular man with the shining face whispered something to the bald man before entering the arena and standing before the youth.

Unsure of what to do, the youth simply stared at the man. The beasts he fought would have blood in their gaze, raise their hackles, or be foaming at the mouth with their claws unsheathed. Their intention to attack was clear, and there was nothing else to do other than to get out of the way or defend yourself. But fighting a man was completely different. The completely shaven, muscled man was grinning like the bald man as he spread his arms wide in a friendly gesture and looked at the youth.

"Come over here, kid. Let's have some fun."

The youth didn't know what this meant. He hesitated. A glance at the muscled man's smiling face, and then a glance at the bald man outside the fence who was watching them.

The bald man kept grinning. "Attack, you idiot. Attack him." He made punching gestures with his white, fat fists.

The youth could understand that gesture, at least. This being the first time he was fighting a man, there was something about the situation that made him hold back at first, but in the end, he followed instructions and lunged at the bald, muscled man.

The man stepped aside with an agility that belied his bulky appearance. The youth turned and lunged again. The older man deftly deflected him with his left palm. Momentum made the youth sprawl to the ground. The muscled man gripped the back of the youth's neck.

Freezing where he was, the moment the muscled man pressed down on the scars on the nape of his neck, he lost all ability to move.

The muscled man grinned. He tossed the youth away like a doll.

The youth slammed against the wooden fence. For a brief moment, his vision blacked out. As he came to and tried to get upright again, he realized his nose was bleeding.

Standing now, he tried to get his wits back by shaking his head. By the time his eyes refocused, the muscled man was right in front of him. The youth had hardly a second to think before his opponent, in a gesture as if to stroke a child's head, spread his palm and slammed it into the youth's temple. The youth stumbled onto the ground again.

Spitting out sand and blood, he stood up again. There had never been a fight that had progressed like this before. In anger, he charged at the man with his fists up.

Like before, the man easily avoided him, even pressing down on the scar as the youth fell again of his own accord. The feeling that he was being mocked only further stoked his fury. But running at the man and making futile attempts at blows was only exhausting him.

Face splattered with blood and sand, the youth swayed as

he stood. He could barely breathe. The muscled man was still grinning as he looked on.

"It's more tiring to miss and hit the air than it is to get some good punches in," he said. "Because it's not just the body that's exhausted, it's the mind."

The youth didn't understand him. All he could see was that the man was making fun of him. Enraged, he forgot all about how tired and out of breath he was. Forming fists with his hands, he attacked once more.

The man again evaded the youth's attacks. He waited for the youth to stumble again, then pressed his knee on the youth's back and brought his fist up to the youth's neck. The moment the youth felt the man's fist, his third knuckle specifically, graze the nape of his neck, the youth heard from somewhere the first, faint sounds of breaking.

Right before his fist could dig into the youth's neck, the muscled man stopped his movement.

The youth caught his breath and waited.

The sound stopped. Nothing happened.

Slowly, the man stood up. He extended a hand but the youth didn't take it. The youth stood up on his own.

Seeing this, the muscled man, yet again, grinned.

The youth could hear the other two men talking as he drank his water and chewed his dried meat.

"As long as he doesn't realize that his opponent is attacking him ..."

"You're saying if we could delay the realization somehow ..."

"But think of what might go wrong ..."

"How? I'm telling you, it never fails to work ..."

In the midst of their talk, the men would smile at the youth if they met his gaze, as if the two had made a prior agreement. The older bald man threw him another scrap of meat. The muscled man made a drinking gesture toward the youth. Seeing his perplexed expression, the muscled man laughed loudly.

IX

A few days later, the youth was sent out to fight once more. But before he stepped into the empty arena, the bald man handed him a liquid in a leather pouch. Opening it without thinking, the youth averted his face from the sudden, sharp smell.

The only liquid he'd known was water. The stuff in the pouch was definitely not water.

He stared at the bald man. As always, he was grinning his grin, and this time he made drinking gestures, throwing his head back with his hand near his mouth.

"Drink up. It's good for you. You've got to make lots of money, right?"

The youth hesitated. The man came closer and grabbed his neck. The moment the youth was helpless, the man poured the stinging liquid in his mouth. The youth coughed and heaved, but the man managed to get almost half of it down his throat.

"Perfect. Now, go! Shoo!" Smirking, the pouch still in his

hand, the man slapped the youth's back and shoved him into the arena.

This time, the youth's opponent was a person. A young man with a fierce expression. His hair was shorn, there was a long scar on his forehead, and his eyes were long, angry slits.

This ferocious young man bounded up to the youth. Thinking he was being attacked, the youth instinctively flinched. But just as his opponent came within striking distance, the man leaped away. His opponent, legs wide apart and swaying back and forth, would approach within an arm's length and jump back, approach and jump back, over and over again.

Watching his opponent do this made the youth feel dizzy. When the opponent, in the midst of this swaying and keeping distance, suddenly hit him in the cheekbones, the youth, who had not even tried to avoid him much less deflect the blow, fell sluggishly to the ground. The people standing around the fence booed him.

He managed to get up. His opponent bounded up to him and kicked his stomach, hard. He managed to break his fall somewhat by stretching out his arms, but the liquid he had drunk suddenly surged from his stomach. When his opponent kicked him one more time, he fell forward and threw up the rest of it.

The green liquid pooled on the ground and dirtied his mouth. For some reason, the crowd roared.

Struggling, he got to his feet. This time, his opponent did not attack but merely waited for him—swaying back and forth like before, watching him.

The youth stared back at him. Having vomited, his insides felt much better. No more dizziness. A little more confident now, he swiftly swung a fist the next time his enemy approached. But the opponent was quicker. The young man with the fierce expression moved as if he were gliding on his feet, dodged under the youth's arm, and slammed the youth's throat with his thumb and forefinger, a quick but effective blow. The wind knocked out of him, the youth began to fall forward. His opponent, seizing the opportunity, sidestepped and made to jab the youth in the neck with his elbow.

Right before the opponent's elbow struck, the youth heard the sound of rocks shattering and steel tearing. For some reason, it wasn't as painful as before.

His opponent's elbow hit something unbelievably hard. The youth heard the sound of the young man's elbow joint breaking and his screams.

The youth sprang to his feet. Reaching out with his right arm to attack, he saw that he still had a cuff on his wrist. So he lowered that arm and with his left arm, grabbed his opponent's neck. The left arm stretching out before him was covered in something hard and glistening, like gray scales, and his hand and fingers looked like they were hewn from rock. That gray hand, looking nothing like a human's, was now wrapped around the ferocious-looking young man's neck, and squeezing.

All these things happened in what felt like a strange slowness. His hand holding up his opponent by his neck, the man's face looked fit to burst, at first turning red, then white, and soon, blue. The youth watched these changes like he were a spectator of the fight.

From the opponent's side, an old man with white hair jumped into the arena. The bald man also came sprinting. This was the first time the youth had seen the bald man without a smile for him. He couldn't make out what the voices of the people shouting at him were saying, but following the orders of the bald man, he dropped his opponent.

His fingers, oddly slow, loosened their grip one by one. His opponent, eyes rolled so far back in agony that the youth could see only the whites, whimpered as he collapsed to the ground. The white-haired old man kept shouting as he dragged the opponent out of the arena. Throughout all this, the audience was in a crazed frenzy, unintelligibly screaming.

Alone in the arena now, the youth stood staring at the chaos outside the ring. The bald man came up to him again, grabbed his right hand, and raised his arm up.

A thunderous roar from the crowd was accompanied by a pelting of small, shining objects into the arena. The man was all grins again as he picked up these sparkling pieces while the youth stared down at his own hands.

They were back to being his normal hands. His arm was back to being what it used to be.

But in that moment, he could finally connect the sound of breaking, the bone-shattering pain, and the gray, stony scales that appeared from the triangular scars along his limbs and back and ribs. He couldn't quite explain what he had understood, but he had a feeling that a very big question of his had just been answered.

The bald man stuffed into his hip pouch the small and sparkling bits and pieces that the people had thrown and still had fistfuls in both hands as he led the youth out of the arena. In no time, the bald man's people had packed up their things and they were on their way out of the village. Even as they made a run for it, the bald man was all smiles.

At the inn where they arrived after a long day's journey, they unpacked in their rooms then ate a large, jovial supper. On the luggage rack of their carriage tied outside, the youth dozed on a pile of straw.

Something prodded him awake. The bald man was fastening a chain to the cuff on his right wrist and locking the chain to something above the youth's head. As the youth tried to get up, the man pressed down on his neck. The youth obediently sat back down.

Holding out a bowl of something, the man said, "Drink."

The youth lowered his head over the bowl to do so but involuntarily turned away. It was something similar to the green stuff he had drunk that morning but with an extra, sharper smell. The dizzy, nauseating feeling came back to him and he frowned.

"Drink!" The man grabbed his neck and shoved his face into the bowl.

Listlessly, the youth tried to resist with his left arm. All that happened was the chain dangling from his right wrist clanged, an irritating sound. With all his might, the man grabbed the youth's neck with one hand and tilted the contents of the bowl into his mouth with the other, forcing him to finish it. Spasms rocked the youth and he coughed violently, but like before, half of it had already made it down his esophagus.

The bald man looked down at him expressionlessly as the

youth coughed and gagged. "If you hadn't drunk that medicine before, you would've killed that bastard. Understand?"

This change in tone was so abrupt that the youth looked up in wonder.

"You were lucky that little shit didn't die and we kept our money and got out of there. Think of what would've happened if you killed him. You'd be finished. Do you hear me?"

The youth kept looking up at him and didn't answer. The man's hand struck the side of the youth's face, hard.

"You hear me?" he shouted again.

Getting slapped out of nowhere made the youth angry, but he couldn't move his body. His face flashed red, but all strength had left his limbs.

"Eat everything I give you from now on, right? Don't throw it up or get clever about it."

Having spat out these last words, the man, teetering slightly, left the carriage and went back into the inn.

X

Ever since the bald man gave him the mysterious liquid to drink and made him fight men, the youth began to feel worse and worse.

The strong-smelling liquid no longer made him vomit so often, but the dizziness and nausea increased. Suppressing the vomit, he tended to be unsteady on his feet in the arena, making him more vulnerable to the blows that rained down upon him. His body was definitely deteriorating, which meant the speed in which he recovered from the effects of the liquid was slowing down.

He knew, of course, that in the last moment, hard scales would sprout from the scars that It had left on him and protect his body from harm. But because he could not think straight, those defenses were slow to come into effect, and with the flagging of his strength and the battering his body was receiving, he could not fight back as hard as he could before.

The day he faced a pale giant with an almost geometrically perfect smile, completely white skin, and red eyes, he thought he would finally die. The red-eyed giant, like a cat playing with a mouse, struck a blow on every part of the youth's body and whipped the crowd into a frenzy. Sometimes the giant would make an aggressive move and the youth would feebly try to counterattack, only to have the giant sidestep out of the way in the last second and bow to the applauding audience, the white giant's red eyes beaming with mirth and confidence. Just as the fight was beginning to seem endless, the giant attempted to strike the final blow on the teetering youth, who was near fainting.

The youth would later remember that just then, he sprouted black wing-like limbs from his back and whacked away the giant that had been lunging for the youth's throat. The giant's body flew out of the arena, and the audience roared with appreciation at this unexpected turn. The wing-like limbs disappeared in the next moment, and the youth felt the blood drain from his face as he began to keel over.

Immediately, the bald man ran up to him and snatched his arm with one hand and propped up his back with the other so that he wouldn't fall. Holding the youth's arm up, the bald man bowed to the audience and gathered the coins that the audience was showering them with as the youth tried not to vomit or fall. The world was spinning, and his insides hurt like they were being twisted.

In the carriage as they pulled out of the village, the bald man counted his coins and cackled.

"Yes, that's the spirit! Keep doing exactly what you did today! Look like you've reached the end and then, bam! Those wings! How did you do that? What's your secret? Oh, who cares, just keep doing what you're doing."

The youth had no idea what the bald man was saying. He did not have the energy for comprehension or concentration. Whenever the carriage shook, his guts felt like they did a flip, and every beat of his heart gave him a pain that felt like something was swelling inside his head.

That night, the youth stared at his right wrist, which was chained to the carriage's luggage compartment, and thought that he needed to escape once more.

XI

It wasn't easy waiting for an opportunity.

From morning until evening, the youth was surrounded by the bald man and his gang, and in the night they all slept together in the carriage. On days when he earned a lot of money, he was left alone in the carriage while the others went drinking, but his right wrist remained chained to the luggage compartment.

More than anything else, however, he was getting weaker and weaker. He no longer had to drink the suspicious liquid in order to feel nauseous; whenever he stood up after sitting for some time or emerged from a dark place into an even slightly brighter one, the world would spin around him. During fights, he had now reached a point where he simply teetered for a while as his opponent landed blow after blow, before he fainted dead away to the boos of the crowd. This prompted the bald man to stop giving him the medicine. But his body had already been damaged, and even as he struggled and tried to choke down his vomit, he was continuously sent out to fight.

It was when the youth could no longer stand up properly on his own that the bald man was finally finished with him. No matter how much the man hit or kicked him or pressed down on his neck, the youth could no longer rise. The bald man spat on him and had one of his underlings carry him over his shoulder into the hills. Once the underling had hacked through quite a bit of forest, he abandoned the youth under a tree and disappeared.

The youth lay on the ground and stared up at the sky. A fragment of blue peeping through the dense covering of the trees.

As he lay there and stared up at the unmoving blue fragment, inhaling the scent of fallen leaves, his endlessly rumbling nausea seemed to ease. A dreamy, relaxed feeling overcame him where he lay completely still.

The blue above him started to gray. It then turned ashen

and rain began to fall. The leaves that covered the ground and his body were mercilessly pelted with fat raindrops.

The rainwater was chilly against his skin. With the rain thickening and the smell of damp earth and leaves growing stronger, he was starting to feel nauseous again. He trembled and almost bounced off the ground as he suddenly sat up and violently vomited what felt like his entire insides. Mustering what little strength that was left in his battered body, he vomited for a long time until there was nothing inside him anymore.

When he was done, he lifted his head and stared up at the sky where the rain was falling from. The raindrops hit his face and slid into his mouth. He drank them in; they were sweet and refreshing.

He got to his feet. It was cold. But the shivers and the pain that had been strangling his guts were dissipating, and were soon gone entirely.

Heading in the opposite direction of where the underling who had brought him here disappeared to, he started to walk.

XII

The youth wandered the mountain forest for four days. Aside from rainwater and some grasses, he ate nothing and continued to walk for a long time.

When he emerged from the forest on the evening of the fourth day and discovered a village, the first thought in his mind was not joy that he had survived but that the village was somehow familiar to him. A rock near the village's entrance, the green-brown earth and gray-barked trees, and the row of houses all came together in an uncanny sense that he had been here before.

But why the village scene was so familiar or where he had seen it before was something that he didn't have the wherewithal to ponder. For four days straight, he had not eaten or slept properly. The things he needed most right now were food and warmth.

He walked into the strangely familiar village.

He still wore the clothes he had worn in the arena. The only thing on his body were the ornate, loose trousers they had given him, and he had no shoes or tunic, just the many scars marking his back and arms, bare to the world.

The sun was melting into different shades of red above the clouds on the horizon, and smoke was rising from the village houses as their inhabitants prepared their evening meals. The smell of cooking made his stomach jump and skip. He walked into the alley between the houses.

Villagers returning from their work stopped in their tracks and stared at him. In the tense silence of their fearful gazes, the youth remembered the day he had escaped It and the cave and come upon the world of people. But unlike back then, there was no grinning man coming up to run and grab his hand.

No one offered him food or warmth. When he tried to enter the houses, the women would take one look at the scars on his ribcage and scream. Farmers holding hoes or rakes would chase him away, making angry faces. He was discouraged. He covered as many of his scars as he could with his arms and hurried out of there.

Once he had escaped the village, he sighed. Should he go to the mountains? He had no clue as to how one survived in the mountains or forest. How to light a fire, where to get food—he didn't even know where to start with such things.

But he had managed to survive on raw meat and greens before. There was no reason why he couldn't continue to do so now. More than anything else, there was no telling what would happen to him if he ever found himself in a village again.

He turned back to the darkening forest and began to walk.

After walking a long time through the trees, in the darkness he saw something like the round roof of a shelter.

It really was a roof. Not only that, there was a whole house underneath it. But seeing how there were no lights on inside despite the dark, he thought it must be abandoned.

He was overjoyed. A place to sleep. While still hungry, night had fallen so he might as well spend the night here and go out to forage for food when the sun came up.

He approached the hut and pushed open the door. The door made a creaking sound as it opened.

From the darkness, a white object approached him. Surprised, he staggered backwards and fell on his behind.

"Brother?" asked the white object.

He didn't know what to say.

XIII

The woman stretched out her arm and fumbled around in the emptiness in front of her.

"Brother?" she asked again.

He tried to calm down. Slowly, he stood up.

"Brother? Why aren't you saying anything?"

The woman approached. Her fingers grazed his cheek.

He froze. Without hesitation, the woman stepped up to him and caressed his face.

He closed his eyes.

... The sweetest moment of his entire life ended with the woman's scream.

"Who are you!"

Her shout frightened him. The woman flailed at the space in front of her as she shouted, "Why are you here! What happened to my brother!"

In the confusion, he grabbed the woman's thrashing wrists. The woman screamed. He turned her around and covered her mouth. As she struggled against him, he dragged her into the house.

As soon as they crossed the threshold, the woman suddenly stopped struggling. He was so surprised that he stopped in his tracks, too.

"Let me go," the woman whispered. "I won't scream, I'll do what you want. Just let me go."

So he let her go.

The woman carefully righted herself. She felt around with her hands and took a step away from him.

"So what do you want from me?" she asked in a cold, low voice. "What have you done to my brother?"

The youth did not know who this brother was. He wasn't there to harm her, either. He wanted to explain this but didn't know how, and he simply took a step closer to her.

He tripped over something and lost his balance. In surprise, he shouted out. And through the darkness, something hard struck the top of his head.

He lost consciousness.

XIV

When he came to, it was bright all around him. He couldn't stand; his hands were tied behind his back.

There was a young man in front of him. A familiar man, strangely enough.

"What are you doing here?" demanded the young man. "What are you doing so far from the cave, and what were you going to do to my sister? Speak!"

The youth could not fully recognize either the young man or his sister. He hadn't come all the way here to do anything. He vigorously shook his head.

The young man was not assuaged. His words and gaze became a shade harsher. "That monster sent you, didn't it? Did it tell you to kill my sister? Or bring her to it?"

The word "monster" made his mind go white.

The young man knew about It. How? The bald man, his gang, the inhabitants of all the villages he had passed by—none of them had ever mentioned It.

Misinterpreting his blank expression, the young man threw a punch at his face.

"Speak!" he shouted. "Why are you here? What were you going to do with my sister?"

Not giving him a chance to answer, he punched the youth's face once more. From the inside of his lip, the youth felt a salty liquid pooling in his mouth.

"Answer me!" The young man struck again.

The youth's vision briefly went black. As he saw the young man's fist rise again, he desperately twisted his body and turned his head. More than being misunderstood as serving It, more than the surprise from meeting someone who knew what It was, he was infuriated by this fist that silenced him every time he was trying to answer.

"Brother, stop that."

The two men turned their heads at the same time. It was then the youth noticed the woman's eyes.

They were a translucent gray. Perhaps she hadn't been born this way, but a thin membrane had formed on her eyes and clouded her vision.

He thought her eyes were beautiful.

The woman was more beautiful than anyone he had ever seen before.

"If he's bad, all we need to do is chase him away. Don't hit him," she said gently.

The young man sighed. "All right. We'll get rid of him." He grabbed the youth by the neck and brought him to his feet. Then, he dragged the youth outside.

The youth kept looking back at the woman. With a worried

expression, she faced the impenetrable space before her, staring with her gray eyes.

The young man dragged the youth out of the house and all the way to the forest path. There, he released his bonds and kicked him, making him stumble onto the ground. As the youth tried to find his balance, the young man kicked him in the stomach.

"Tell that monster," said the young man as he watched the youth writhe in pain on the ground, "that my sister is off limits. I don't know what is going on, but my sister will never be a part of that!"

And the young man turned to go back to his house.

The youth grabbed his ankle.

Turning, the young man kicked the youth in the face. Coughing, the youth collapsed once more and spat out the blood that pooled in his mouth. But when the young man turned toward home again, the youth grabbed his ankle once more.

In truth the man was frightened, but he didn't kick the youth this time. Instead, he stared down as if there was something he hadn't noticed before.

"What is wrong with you?"

The youth carefully looked up at the young man. He gestured putting food in his mouth.

"You want food?"

The youth nodded.

Nonplussed, the young man gave a snort of laughter. And he lifted his foot to trample the youth again.

The youth covered his head with his hands but didn't make

to escape. He lay there before the young man in the most self-denigrating pose possible, beseeching him.

"Are you a fool? You come to our house looking for a sacrifice and now you want to be fed?"

Looking up, the youth vigorously shook his head. He made eating gestures with his hands again.

The young man looked down at him for a long time. "Maybe you really are a fool."

The only answer the youth could give him was to keep miming eating.

The young man roughly brought the youth to his feet. "We're only doing this once," he said as he dragged him along. "Just once. When you've eaten, leave. Go far away and never come back."

XV

The youth never strayed far from the house the gray-eyed woman and her brother lived in.

When the woman brought him food, he gobbled it up quickly. Her brother took him to the shed after his meal. Without any explanation, as if there was no need for any, the brother attached a chain to the youth's right cuff and fastened it tightly to a rafter of the shed using a heavy lock.

"Don't think you can do whatever you like with us."

The brother left.

In the morning, the brother came back and released him, but the youth sat lingering in the shed.

Only when the brother tried to shoo him away did he

mime with his hands and feet that he had nowhere else to go. When the brother became angry and used his fists, the youth didn't try to avoid the blows. He fell to the ground and acted as pitifully as possible, begging to stay with them.

"Tell me the truth. Where are you from?"

At this question, all the youth could do was shake his head as hard as he could.

"Why are you here? What do you plan to do to my sister?"

He was struck with blows along with each question, but all the youth did was shake his head. The brother became convinced he was at least partially a fool.

At first, the youth mostly sat in the shed. Then one day, the brother dragged him out of it. Instead of his thin, outlandish trousers he was given a thick, practical pair along with a tunic, and taken to the forest. Of his elaborate costume or the cuff on his right wrist, the brother never asked a thing.

He followed the brother around gathering mushrooms and fruit. The brother hunted small animals as well. The youth knew nothing about hunting or anything else that was the slightest bit useful in putting food on the table. And because he was bad at everything, he was regularly beaten by the brother. Even as he was beaten and insulted, he never tried to avoid the blows or escape.

He did know one thing, and that was which greens were edible; he presented whatever fragrant herb he found to the woman along with the mushrooms and fruit. The woman avoided him and generally tried to keep her distance, but when he offered these gifts, she seemed at least a little pleased.

On the rare occasions the brother was in a good mood while they foraged, he talked to the youth or even hummed a song. The youth nodded along or shook his head to communicate his understanding. In the evenings, after dinner, the brother would take him back to the shed and chain him up as a matter of course, locking the shed behind him. The youth obediently did as he was told by the brother.

The brother hadn't noticed this, but there was a gap at the end of the rafter he was chained to, which meant the youth could jiggle his chain off the end of it. Even after the youth had slipped the chain out and released his right-hand cuff, he never left the shed. Instead, he wandered around, looking at the stack of hay, the ropes, planks, and various farming implements he hadn't an inkling how to use. One evening, he overheard from outside the shed's window the woman and her brother talking about him.

"We can't keep him forever in that shed like some beast," said the woman.

"He escaped from the monster," said the man in an ominous voice. "He must never be sheltered inside the house. And we can't keep him in the shed for too long, either."

"He escaped from the monster? How do you know?"

"Look at his scars. What else engraves such scars on its sacrifices?"

The youth felt his breath knocked out of him. But he tried not to utter a sound as he continued to eavesdrop.

"He's either here to bring back a sacrifice to replace himself or he's out for revenge. Either way, it doesn't bode well for us."

"Then what are we to do?" asked the woman in a trembling voice.

"Don't worry. Even animals like that have their use in this world. I know someone who will take him somewhere far away."

"Who is that? Where would he take him?" the woman asked in a worried voice.

"That's for me to know. You don't have to trouble yourself with that knowledge. It's late, we should go back inside."

That was the end of the conversation.

The youth finally realized why the brother seemed so familiar to him. When he had escaped from the cave and arrived at the first village he had found and the bald man had come to get him, the brother was the young man who had been talking to the bald one.

He could not return to fighting in the arenas. He would not last long.

But he had to know. What was this monster? And why did it need sacrifices?

And why had he been selected for that sacrifice?

While he was mulling these questions over, the door of the shed creaked open.

Wordlessly, the gray-eyed woman entered.

XVI

The youth was so surprised that he stood there without making a sound.

Then he realized he had released the chain her brother had

tied to him without permission. Quickly, he dashed back to where he was supposed to be and tried to sling the chain back on the rafter. It made a loud sound as it fell to the ground instead. He was picking it up when he remembered that the woman was blind.

"Are you there?"

The woman smiled. He nodded but then realized she could not see and chastised himself inwardly. Instead, he moved the chain so it made a sound.

"Did you really escape from the monster?"

He pulled at the chain again. It reverberated loudly in the shed.

"Are you here to exact your revenge on me, then?"

He couldn't understand her. All he could do was stare into her gray, pupil-less eyes.

"You were sacrificed to the monster in my stead, weren't you?"

He was becoming more and more confused. Understanding nothing, he continued to look into her white face.

The woman took a step toward him. Before he could move away, she gently placed a hand on his wrist.

Her fingers were long and slender and soft. He remembered how her hand had felt as it caressed his face when he first came here, how she had mistaken him for her brother.

"Please sit," she said. "I will tell you everything."

XVII

Once upon a time. All legends start this way.

Once upon a time, there was a place plagued by a disease every few years. The disease was thought to be from a monster that lived in the highest cave of the highest mountain in that region, a monster resembling a large crow, which flew down once every few years when it was hungry to devour the crops and trees. The villagers believed it exhaled poison whenever it opened its mouth, which meant any person or animal in its vicinity would get sick and die.

They decided to prevent the monster from getting hungry and coming out of its cave by giving it a sacrifice. According to a sorcerer, the best sacrifice was a prepubescent child. Whenever the air became tepid and the people and beasts of the village began to fall ill, the people left a child in the cave on the mountain. This practice persisted, and even when there was no plague, when someone was sick, the villagers sometimes took a child that had no family to the cave and prayed for the afflicted to get better.

"It was not a plague year, but I was born with a sickness," the woman said in a soft voice. "I became blind from it. If nothing had been done for me, the disease would've spread all over my body—I would've become deaf and mute, unable to move on my own, unable to breathe, and ended up having to die a torturous death. At least, according to the sorcerer."

Her voice became even softer. "So my father and brother found and kidnapped an orphan child from outside the village and sacrificed him to the cave."

She whispered, "Was that you?"

He had no answer.

The woman waited. Because he said nothing, she asked, "Are you still there?"

He barely managed to give the chain a shake.

The woman said, "I did not know such things had been done. I only learned later, when I heard others talking. I was a child myself, but to learn that another child had been killed to save me … That has always been a great source of sadness."

He made no sound.

Softly, the woman spoke again. "After sacrificing the child, my father died in an accident a short while later. I thought that was the revenge the sacrificed child had taken on our family. But the real person who deserved to die was me."

The youth stroked the chain and could only gaze at the woman silently.

"So … if you want revenge, do whatever you want."

She stopped talking.

They sat in silence. The woman spoke again. "Are you still there?"

He threw the chain to the ground, wrapped the woman's white face in his hands, and kissed her lips.

XVIII

The next morning, the woman's brother opened the door to the shed to find her sitting alone, in tears.

"He's gone to kill the monster," she said through her sobs. "He said it wasn't my fault, that I did nothing wrong. That what made the people sick in both body and soul, that what made them harm the children of others was the monster, that he must therefore kill the monster, that he would kill the monster ..."

The brother took his sister in his arms and consoled her before taking her back to the house. Of the news he just heard, he didn't know whether to be joyful or dread what was coming to the village.

XIX

Relying on old memories, the youth made his way up the mountain. The words he had heard from the woman echoed endlessly inside his head.

"An orphan child from the outside the village." He was a little crestfallen with those words. But if the woman's brother had been there when he had been kidnapped, he could at least learn where he'd been found, and under what circumstances. From that scrap of knowledge, he might be able to find his home, his parents, maybe even his name.

But that didn't help him think of a way to kill It. He hadn't set out with a clear plan. But then again, never in his life had he made a plan or had an inkling as to what to do.

To not be caught and consumed by It. To survive somehow and return.

Just like when he was trapped in the cave before, survival was his objective and plan.

And that was what he vowed when he stood at the mouth of the cave.

He entered.

XX

Because he was used to the light of the sun outside, the complete darkness of the cave briefly disoriented him. He slowly began feeling his way forward.

How strange a person's fate was. When she was little, the woman had had an older brother and a father. A family that worried over her health, a home, a life. All that had been granted to the youth was this damp, moldy cave and its hard rocks, the handcuffs and manacles on a chain, and a stake attached to that chain. Every person has only one childhood, and instead of being full of hopes or dreams, his had been crushed by the fight for survival. He never once imagined in all his years spent in the cave that a different childhood from the one that had been accorded to him might have been possible.

And now that he was back inside the cave, senses that had been long dormant revived inside him. The cave was his world, and whether he liked to or not, he remembered every wrinkle in the rock and rise or depression in the floor.

If he was this used to it, perhaps he himself was a part of this cave …

Just as he was thinking this, his hand touched the iron stake.

From the woman's shed, the youth had brought the chain that the woman's brother had linked to his right cuff. Now that he had arrived in the prison of his childhood, he crouched down next to the stake like he used to. This was his place, and it had been kept empty for him. If he were lucky, no one would ever have to take his place.

The distant white spot that was the cave's entrance was blocked by a huge black form.

The youth lifted his chin and stared into the dark.

Never while he lived in the cave did he manage to see what It looked like. Back then, It would appear suddenly, blocking the entrance of the cave, and in the next moment It would be on the youth's back, crushing his limbs with its wings and talons, piercing him between his bones with its sharp beak.

Like previous times, It tried to climb on his back. Realizing that the youth was not a child and was wearing clothes, It, as if mocking him, ripped away at his tunic. The talons slicing through his flesh as well as his garments made him want to scream, but he held his silence.

It never pierced him in the same place twice. There were scars along his back, limbs, and ribs where It had violated him before, and if It wanted to find an unspoiled spot, it would have to spend some time looking. The youth was counting on that moment.

It finished ripping off his tunic, pressed down on his neck, and positioned its beak. The youth, tense with the fear of what might happen next, briefly closed his eyes.

As expected, It saw the scars on his neck and drew back its beak. As it followed the scars down his back and along his arms and ribs, It tried to rip his trousers. The youth twisted his upper body and swung the chain connected to his right handcuff.

In the dark, the chain made a heavy, threatening sound as it whipped through the damp air and smashed against an unseen object. The youth couldn't tell what it had hit, but he heard a hard and clear shattering sound and a scream that shook the interior of the cave, followed by a hideous smell. Aiming right below the source of the odor, he swung his chain once more.

The resulting scream almost deafened him as it shook the walls. And in the very next moment, his chain was wrapped around a talon, and he was flying through the air.

It was beautiful. He couldn't help thinking so when, for the first time, he could clearly see It by the light of the sun. It was truly, monstrously beautiful.

In the sunlight, It was not black but dark gray. Its ashen feathers gleamed like well-forged iron, a cold and lifeless sheen. Its talons and beak were silver, and in the middle of that silver beak was a short but deep, red gash. The youth surmised this was where his chain had hit.

Beside the beak was an icy blue eye staring down at him. That shade of blue, to someone seeing it for the first time, was shockingly deep and clear, and cruel.

He wound his chain tighter around its feet and tried to hoist himself up. But one of the links of the chain he dangled from came into contact with the sharp talons and was sliced into two. Even if he survived the fall like the time he escaped from It, there would be no point in having come all this way if he let It fly off to somewhere far away. He desperately clung onto the silver claws of It and tried to climb up on the monster without getting scratched.

Just then, It lowered its head and bit down on him.

When he felt the steely beak close down from his ribcage to his legs, he was certain he was about to die. But It did not swallow him or shake him off into the air. As painful as it was, he wasn't being bitten down on strong enough for his bones to break—this could only mean It was trying to take him somewhere.

The minute he thought this, It tossed him in the air and caught him again in its beak. Now the youth lay on his back facing the sky and staring straight into the blue eye of It.

If beasts could show emotions in their eyes, the emotion that the youth would have discerned at that moment would have been clearly one of satisfaction. But being different from people, beasts do not derive satisfaction from scaring or torturing others. The question they ask of any other animal is whether it will kill it or be killed by it. As long as they can prevent themselves from being killed while having prey in their grasp, animals don't need to concern themselves with the feelings of their prey; simply the fact of having prey in their grasp is enough satisfaction.

It made a wide arc in the air. It was flying back to the cave.

Without hesitation, the youth swung his right arm, hard. The chain connected to his right cuff smashed directly into the icy blue eye of It, and the half-sliced link gave way, leaving a fragment of the chain lodged in the eye.

It gave out a shriek that shook Heaven and Earth as it banked to one side. In its sudden, blind pain, It darted toward a cliff on the mountain where the cave was and crashed.

XXI

He couldn't understand how he was still alive. But buried as he was in broken branches, scattered leaves, grasses, and brambles, his breath still hadn't left his body.

As he tried to get up, he felt a jolt through the right side of his body. He couldn't move his right leg. Grabbing one of the thicker branches around him, he used it as a crutch to slowly and carefully stand up.

The behemoth had crashed against the cliff and broken its neck.

Its eyes were devoid of life; its giant beak still gleamed silver in the light. A wingspan wide enough to wrap over the ridge of the mountain, but the stiff feathers were so clumped and crushed that they looked like rough cloth.

He stood still and stared at the dead bird.

The bird was dead, and it would never steal again, nor would anything be stolen from it. The only evidence the bird ever existed would be the scars on the youth's body from when he had been its prey.

A realization that somehow saddened the youth.

Without knowing why, he found himself wishing the bird would revive, that it hadn't died so easily, as he stood there and gazed into its blue eye.

Then, he began to limp back toward the village where the woman was waiting.

XXII

Dusk was settling by the time he arrived at the village. The red sun had fragmented and its pieces were dissolving into the spaces between the iridescent clouds, a sight that he would never tire of.

He took the path through the village and began walking up to the forest in the mountains beyond. There were no lights seen from the road. The woman's brother had gone out to the forest and hadn't returned, and the woman was blind so she didn't need the light. That was what he told himself as he hurried his pace.

At the threshold of the hut, before he opened the door, he called out the woman's name. He didn't want to barge in and surprise her.

No sounds came from within. He pushed open the hut door.

The woman had been sitting at the table, and she stood up as she heard the door open. Approaching him, she held out her hand. In his gladness to see her, he also reached out for her hand.

The moment his fingertips brushed hers, the woman transformed into thousands of water droplets and scattered into thin air.

XXIII

Overwhelmed by what had just happened, he stood frozen by the door, his hand still stretched out for hers.

Behind him, a cry as if from a beast. He turned.

The woman's brother charged at him with a hunting knife.

The youth sidestepped just in time.

He tried to explain, but the brother did not want to listen. In truth, the youth did not understand what had happened, either.

The brother's momentum carried him past the youth. He turned and rushed at the youth again while uttering his cry.

The youth grabbed the man's arm and gripped his wrist, trying to make him drop the knife, but it was impossible to overpower the man, who was filled with mad strength. No matter how much the youth resisted, the man's blade inched toward his neck.

Its tip touched him. The youth felt it pierce his skin, and blood beginning to flow.

And in that moment, the youth saw his hand that was gripping the man's wrist was turning into a steely gray.

The man's wrist began bending back in an impossible angle. White bone popped out from his skin. The man screamed and fell to the floor, clutching his broken arm.

The youth stared down at the man. Incandescent rage had vanished from the man's eyes. They were soon flooded with fear.

That was the last thing the youth remembered.

XXIV

When he came to again, it was morning.

The woman and her brother's hut had vanished without

a trace. Where the shed had once stood were what looked like the man's scattered remains, along with oceans of blood. Finding it unbearable to look at, he turned his head and quickly left the scene.

When he came down the mountain to the village, he saw that it was in ruins.

Where yesterday there had been houses and people passing by, now stood an old tree, hundreds of years old, standing there as it had since time immemorial. Where there had once been a fence thick with vines and a blacksmith's, was now just a field of dried grass. The inhabitants were almost all gone. Two or three stragglers, wandering the scene with dazed expressions, took one look at him, turned white with fear, and disappeared from his sight.

He despaired.

He hadn't wanted revenge. At least, not this kind of revenge. He simply had not known that the village's survival had hinged solely on the existence of It.

The absurdity of the conclusion made him feel helpless. The strangers who stole his childhood with their sorcerer and beliefs, the despondent life he had lived on the brink of death, it had all been meaningless in the end. Mourning his years of suffering and despair, he stood there in the ruins of the village and wept.

And once his tears had finally ceased, he began to walk toward the rising sun, in search for that place in this world where his life was waiting for him.

Home Sweet Home

"Surely you must know that it's only good manners to compensate me thirty million won in this situation, if you know what I mean, dear." The owner of the blood-sausage stew restaurant spoke to the young woman and the young woman's husband in an oddly unsettling confusion of polite and informal speech.

The restaurant owner's husband chimed in, "You young people don't seem to know the ways of the world very well. But if you can't do this little thing, it can become a miserable life for all of us." He glared at them meaningfully as he said this.

The man in black, standing next to the restaurant owner and her husband, nodded. Then, wordlessly, he smiled.

"Excuse me," said the young woman's husband to the three of them, "but the exchange of a 'premium' is only a traditional practice between renters, is it not? It has nothing to do with the landlord in official legal terms. And thirty million won is not a small sum of money. Would *you* be so willing to part with it?"

Even as the young woman was half-listening to her husband's trembling voice as he used the proper honorifics and formal speech while trying to reason with the extortionists and their black-clad "assistant" (or, rather, their hired thug), she was watching the child. The child was in the corner of the store, sweeping her fingers along the wall, then fiddling with the pot of fake flowers by the door, but she did not venture outside. When their eyes met, the child smiled. The young woman returned the smile.

On the seventh year of her marriage, she managed to repay all her loans. Her in-laws had helped out a little (or a lot, really), but in the end, she had paid them off. Hearing that the best way to raise your children in one place was to have a larger home to begin with, she may have gone in over her head when she bought their first apartment, and she had to quickly adjust to the bitter feeling of going to the banks and giving them almost every cent they earned for seven long years. But it was money well spent in the end. After those seven years, the apartment finally belonged in its entirety to herself and her husband, and she decided they should sell it and move to a neighborhood which was cheaper and quieter. And so, on the eighth year of their marriage, she bought a mixed-use building in a cheap part of town.

She hadn't been entirely happy with it. "Pleased" would've been an overstatement. The times she and her husband had made surveying expeditions into various parts of the city had been fun. The neighborhood they had settled on was quiet, not too expensive, and most of the people who lived there had the aura of calm that came from having been there for decades. As most of the inhabitants were rather elderly, the real estate agent (whose sign still used the old-fashioned term bokdeokbang, or "fortune-gainer") seemed somewhat perplexed that such a young couple would come in itching to buy an entire building with cash.

But the woman was finally happy. How thrilling it was to buy one's own place with one's own money for the first time! Not to mention the fact that she wanted to leave their apartment as soon as possible. There, from the parking lot to the elevators, every time she ran into a neighbor there was tedious talk of land prices, house prices, petitions from the wives' association, and exhortations to attend meetings of said association, exhortations that bordered on harassment.

She knew she was not "being clever." Where these people learned such tricks to being clever, she didn't know, nor did she want to know. Making as much money as quickly as possible, buying a larger house and more expensive car, sending your children to expensive English-language kindergartens and competitive private schools, and going on expensive family vacations abroad every season may seem like a prosperous life to some. But it wasn't the life she wanted. She wanted a quiet and peaceful life and sought a modest yet warm community where she could live out her days in harmony with her neighbors. She thought she had finally found such a place.

Except she did not like the building from the start.

It's an old building in an old neighborhood, she thought as she kept trying to convince herself. It was the price of an apartment, and if she wanted to buy a whole building, small as it was, there was no choice but to go with a more dilapidated one, no matter how uninspired the location. The building was much cheaper than most other places, was situated at the entrance to an alley that led to a main road, and wasn't so far from the subway or bus stops—so perhaps it wasn't that uninspired a location, either. After briefly consulting with her husband, and a short moment of hesitation, she made her decision to buy.

The real problems began after the woman and her husband bought the building.

It had four floors aboveground and a larger-than-expected basement. There was a café on the first floor and a small rented-out office on the second. The third floor had just lost its tenant and was empty, and the fourth floor had been where the owner had lived according to the "fortune-gainer." Saying it would be improper to barge into an apartment where someone was still living, the fortune-gainer showed them the empty third floor instead. To not ask questions or demand answers and simply look at what was being shown before signing on the dotted line was a fatal mistake that even rookies like them could've avoided.

After the former owner moved out, they finally entered the fourth floor to see not only piles upon piles of trash but piles upon piles of rat droppings as well, and a few meagre pieces of furniture rotting where they stood. Everything about the place screamed abandonment. It was unbelievable to the woman that this had been "where someone was still living" until recently. The second she began to pick up the trash, cockroaches came pouring out underfoot. The deluge was more than she could stomp with her foot, and her initial attempts to whack them brought out a bevy of surprised rats. She screamed and declared a retreat.

The problem was not solved by fumigation sessions with exterminators. They had already come in four times to fight against the horde of roaches and rats while she had been practically breaking her back cleaning up. Fed up, she called the former building owner.

The owner did not pick up. She dialed again, but after a few rings, the line cut off by itself. She called several more times out of spite, but just as she was about to give up, there was a voice on the other end of the line. "Hello?" Glad to finally get through, the woman explained who she was and tried to summarize the situation, but the moment she mentioned the word "building," the old woman at the other end suddenly screamed obscenities so loudly that the younger woman thought her eardrum would burst and abruptly hung up before the young woman had a chance to speak again.

That was enough to quash any desire to call again. Instead, the woman called the fortune-gainer.

What an odd day the woman was having vis-à-vis phone calls. The fortune-gainer was out showing a home to a client, said the auntie who had only picked up after the phone had rung for a long time. The woman figured she was the wife of the fortune-gainer. They had met only once before.

"Don't be like that," said the fortune-gainer's wife when she heard the woman's story. "You're younger, you must be the one to be patient. That old woman is a pitiful person herself.

Her husband died early and her only child, a son, went out on a delivery helping his mother's business and hurt his head in a motorcycle accident ... So young, such a waste, he wasn't even married, poor thing ..."

The fortune-gainer's wife sighed. "After that happened, the old woman went a little strange ... She closed the restaurant she'd run nearly all her life and left with her son. To some Christian retreat. The building was all she owned at the time but she got rid of even that at a pittance ..."

This surprised the woman. "She went on a retreat? So ... she didn't live in the fourth-floor apartment?"

"I haven't seen her in a long time. She did seem to come back every once in a while to fetch clothes and such—"

"How long has it been since she left?" she asked.

"I don't know," said the fortune-gainer's wife calmly. "Three or four years?"

After she hung up, the woman found it hard to sort out her feelings. Now she understood why the building had been so much cheaper than others in the same neighborhood. And perhaps a little of why her neighbors would give her and her husband anxious glances. All she had thought at the time was that the old people were simply resentful that young people had bought an entire building and were moving in.

Now there was nothing more she could gain by chasing this up with the former owner. After about ten bouts with the exterminator in the first month alone, the rat and roach problem was finally under control. There had been an incident where the rats, pushed out of their refuge, had swarmed through the café on the first floor. This had upset the café owner who declared he was moving out. The woman was worried that she would have no renters left and the building would end up empty, but a new renter appeared quite swiftly. A blood-sausage stew shop stank a lot more than a café, but the woman was relieved. Finally, she and her husband could retrieve the boxes stored at her mother's and move into the fourth floor of this building of their own.

The child liked the basement. The woman thought this was because there were many things to look at and play with. She had been told it was all stuff that had been left behind by the former third-floor renter. Whatever this mysterious person did, the basement was filled with costumes, shoes, and props one might see in a play. When she switched on the light and entered the space for the first time, the sight of the child jumping out of the ranks of lined-up mannequins in freakish gowns made her jump back in surprise. But once she had the exterminators confirm that no rats or roaches were hiding in the basement and she changed the lightbulbs, the basement didn't seem so scary anymore. She actually began to enjoy walking through the rows of mannequins and their unbelievably ostentatious clothing and shoes and mysterious props, the likes of which modern city-dwellers rarely got to see, brightly illuminated by fluorescent lights.

"Weird," said the exterminator after his inspection. "Normally you'd have rats come up from the basement to the upper floors. But this building has it upside-down." He tilted his head. "The rats and insects are mostly on the top floor and the basement is as clean as a whistle. I've never seen a basement crammed with so many things and yet not have a single bug."

The exterminator's words were reassuring. She allowed the child to drag her down to the basement where she would be shown yet another fascinating new costume or prop—although the woman had been sure that she had examined everything in the basement by then—and make the appropriate exclamations, sharing in the child's fun.

The older the neighborhood, the harder it is to stake your own territory. The woman experienced "turf" politics for the first time.

Someone in the night kept leaving scratch marks on their old car, a hand-me-down from her husband's oldest brother. At first it had been a couple of marks on the driver-side door. The next night, the entire driver-side door was scratched up. A scratch so long that it wrapped around the vehicle appeared the next morning, and on the fourth night, both side mirrors were smashed. A week later, someone had slashed the rear tires.

She and her husband could guess at the perpetrator and his motive. After moving in, they parked their car on the street in front of their building as they were entitled to, but a man insisting that the space was rightfully his began to menace them. He was a young man in his early thirties who lived in an old house at the end of the alley. The third generation to live there, he bragged that his family had once owned the entire neighborhood and thus, the street-parking space at the entrance of the alley actually belonged to him—"facts" arrogantly conveyed to them in a commanding voice.

Whether the land had once been the man's family's or not, the situation was completely different now. The space in front of the building was prioritized for its inhabitants by law, a space the woman and her husband paid parking and zoning permission fees for. Of course, such reasonable explanations had no effect on the man who lived down the alley.

"If you've moved into someone else's neighborhood, you should follow their rules!" he shouted as he jabbed a finger at them. "You can't come in here and mess up the order of our neighborhood!"

Neither the woman nor her husband could understand how parking in the spot that was designated for them and they were paying for was "messing up the order of the neighborhood." Her husband suggested they simply ignore him, and she agreed. And it was around three days after this confrontation when someone began to damage their car at night.

The woman had felt anxious when the very first scratches appeared on the door. Her husband had simply laughed it off, but after the side mirrors were smashed and the tires were slashed, her husband's expression also darkened. The woman and her husband installed CCTV cameras on their building wall, right next to a streetlamp. They would need proof if they were to ever seek legal recourse.

The mere presence of the cameras would solve many of their problems, the CCTV technician was at pains to emphasize. And his words proved true at first, as nothing happened for the next few days.

But a week later, the woman picked up the phone to receive a summons from the police: someone was pressing charges against her husband.

That someone turned out to be, of course, the man who lived down the alley. The charge was assault. According to the man, he was on his way home late at night after work and passing by the car that was parked in the contested space, when the woman's husband leaped out of the car and assaulted him. He had allegedly struck the young man with his car door, picked him up, smashed his face on the hood of the car, and slammed his fingers in the door, inflicting massive injuries. The man did have wounds all over his face along with a bandage around his head, and his right hand was in a cast.

Such violence was completely out of character for the husband, so the woman knew the accusation was false. At any rate, on the date and hour the man claimed to have been assaulted, her husband had been sleeping at home next to her and they hadn't gone out that evening. As she and her husband denied all accusations, the man began to scream and hop up and down despite his injuries, but then came the couple's secret weapon: the CCTV footage.

Since no incidents had happened in the past few days, the woman and her husband had simply stored the footage without bothering to review it. But the footage, which they all watched with the detective in charge of the case, revealed something very strange.

The man came up to the car from down the alley. From his direction and manner, he was clearly doing the opposite of what he had claimed earlier—walking past the car on his way home. There was some kind of tool in his hand. The darkness and screen resolution made it impossible to make out what it was exactly.

The man approached the car. The moment his hands touched the vehicle, the car door sprang open. It really did look like the door had been intentionally opened to slam the man in his face. The man lost his balance and fell on his behind. As he tried to get up again, the door slammed into his face once more. Over and over, it kept doing the same thing as the man attempted to get up multiple times.

Then his body was upright—not balanced on his own feet, but seemingly hoisted up as if by an invisible assailant. His head crashed onto the hood. The man struggled, kicking the tires as he did so, but his head crashed again and again into the hood of the car until he finally managed to gain his balance. That was when the driver-side door slammed him once again. The man grabbed the edge of the door with his right hand for balance, and the door shut with his hand still in it. He freed his hand and fell on the ground, clutching his right hand. The camera did not have a microphone, but the man's pain was clear from his silent, wide-open mouth.

The detective turned to the man. "So where exactly in this videotape did an assault take place?"

The only person in the footage, from beginning to end, had been the man. No matter how you tried to spin it, all it looked like was the man engaging in self-harm using the car belonging to the woman and her husband.

The detective spoke again. "And just how did you open someone else's car? Did you steal their keys?"

The man began shouting his objections, but a glance at the detective's suspicion-filled gaze brought him down to a mumble. "But, but I was sure that someone came out of the car and—"

"What person? What person out of where?" the detective cut in with a rough voice. The man attempted to say something, but the detective didn't give him a chance.

"So you thought you'd extort these poor people by pretending they beat you up, is that it? Is pressing charges some kind of game to you?"

"But I'm positive that someone had—"

"What someone? Where? You still dare to speak such lies when there's CCTV proof right in front of you?"

The detective was having none of it. He mentioned that extortion was a criminal offence. But the woman and her husband, saying they all had to live in the same neighborhood, requested leniency for the man, who continued muttering that he was sure someone had been in the car even as they exited the station. But his mumbling was now shot through with fear.

A few days later, they learned that the man had been charged for attempted extortion. And when the woman was on her way home from the supermarket, she saw the man's expensive sedan parked on the street—its interior filled with heavy rocks and its tires slashed to shreds. The sight was so chilling that she rushed into their building without a second glance behind.

The man never again bothered them about parking in front of their building. Even when they ran into him in the neighborhood, he simply turned his head and went the other way. They could hear him grumble about how they had ruined his day by committing the offence of simply being visible, but neither she nor her husband dignified him with a response.

The child liked to play in the building. She'd go exploring in the different rooms, and whenever she seemed to have momentarily disappeared, she could always be found in the basement.

And that was all she liked to do. She didn't seem to want to go outside much. The woman tried several times to take her to the supermarket or go for a walk around the neighborhood, but the child always shook her head in refusal. The woman didn't press the issue.

They had a hard time finding a renter for the third floor.

Collecting rent was the only way her husband and she could have a steady income. The third floor had been empty since before they had moved in, and as time passed, she began to feel more and more anxious about its vacancy.

"Why don't we remodel it," suggested her husband.

"Wouldn't that be expensive? We'd have to get a permit, too. What if no one wants it even after we remodel?"

Her husband, however, was more confident than she was. "My friend said he would use it as an office. He also said he knows someone who can get us a discount on the remodeling. The interior designer went to our school. She'll take care of the permits and everything."

The woman had met her husband at a student club in college. He was older than her. The friend he mentioned was also someone she knew from the club. The interior decorator who would take charge of the remodeling claimed she too had briefly been a member of the same club. After meeting her and hearing her name, the woman had the feeling that she had, indeed, seen her before. As the construction began and her husband's friend and the interior designer and their workers made a lot of bustle and noise on the third floor, the heightened energy seemed to infect the woman's husband as well. He, who had never lifted a finger to help her clean after they moved in, was all excited about remodeling the office his friend was going to use, gushing to her about every little step of their progress. The woman had no idea he'd be so enthused about anything having to do with taking care of the building and welcomed this development.

The child fervently hated the fact that a new tenant was moving into the third floor. The noise drifting up to the fourth floor must've been unbearable as she was now always going down into the basement to hide.

The woman also found it hard to tolerate having the stairs constantly covered in dust and the sounds of drills and hammers coming from below. Aside from when her husband called for her or the second-floor tenant lodged the occasional complaint, the woman also spent most of her time playing with the child in the basement.

In addition to the red, ornate robes on the mannequins and the shoes with toes so pointy they seemed impossible to put on, the child was good at finding all sorts of odd metal boxes in the basement. These boxes occasionally had locks or sealing mechanisms with keys attached to them, but even with the keys, it was difficult to figure out how to open them. The child handed over one box. The woman awkwardly played around with it, and when the box double-locked itself in her hands with a loud *clunk*, she nearly jumped out of her skin. The child laughed brightly. At first, the woman found it unsettling when the cold lump of iron suddenly went *clunk* in her hands apparently on its own accord. But watching the child laugh as she locked the odd-looking boxes one by one, she forgot that strange feeling and laughed along with her.

The seemingly endless remodeling efforts finally came to an end and her husband's friend moved into the office. Despite the great lengths they'd gone to redo the third floor and how spacious the office was, the friend seemed to have no employees; it all struck the woman as peculiar. Her husband explained that it was because his business was just starting out and he praised the friend for being cautious with his overheads. Her husband, as if he were an employee himself, was always in the office. Whenever she peeped in, he was always sitting across from the friend with a narrow desk between them, both talking urgently into their phones. Occasionally, the husband's friend would call her down to the office and offer her a dark-colored drink. The drink was so sour and tart that she could only manage two sips the first time in the name of good manners before giving up. Her husband's friend claimed the drink was made from some government-subsidized crop in Europe and had cancer-fighting, antioxidant, and anti-aging properties, going on a long rant using terms she couldn't understand. Her husband nodded along to the friend's spiel until his phone rang and he immediately answered it.

Before even three months had passed, her husband's friend vanished with their seed capital. In the office, aside from the small desk and the plush "CEO's chair," were crates upon crates of juice containers. She assumed they were the drink the friend had kept pushing on her. Emblazoned on the containers' packaging was a picture of tiny blue berries. The same berries that were rotting away in a fridge in the corner of a room.

"We still have his security deposit, so we haven't lost that much money," said her husband nonchalantly. "And he left all this product behind. It's 200,000 won a box ... Think of all the money we can make selling them."

Vowing to minimize their losses as much as possible, he called up everyone he knew and spewed the same information about the blue fruit's anti-cancer properties, marketing them as best he could. But the thought of all the boxes stacked on the third floor made the woman despair that he would ever sell them all.

Then, the phone calls began.

If only they hadn't tried to remodel, if only they hadn't rented it out to her husband's friend ... These regrets crossed her mind again and again.

She knew there was no use in agonizing over the past. But the regrets revisited her anyway. It would've been the same for anyone else in her position.

He told her he had taken out a loan of twenty million won. At least he had only "invested" it in his friend's business and did not put his own name on the business or be a guarantor to his friend's debts.

She wanted to cry. She wanted to shout. Seven years of her life had been put into repaying her debt, working late into the night and saving her meagre salary, living a humble life—and now, here she was right back where she started. No matter the amount, the word "loan" made her eyes go dark.

Her husband had pursued an "alternative lifestyle" that was "free of the fetters of capitalism." The woman herself, when she was in college, had considered the conformist pressures of getting good grades, building a resume, and landing a job in some big corporation to be tedious and distasteful and had thought the life her husband wanted dovetailed with hers. They got married as soon as she graduated, and she got a job right after. She learned quickly that an "alternative lifestyle" meant nothing without a detailed, concrete plan, and living "free of the fetters of capitalism" meant working for places that didn't pay their workers on time. As she worried about realizing this alternative lifestyle in the real world, she crumbled away under the pressures of working at a company in the non-profit sector that was run not by the normal labor of workers, but through their unrequited sacrifices. Meanwhile, her husband, who was her upperclassman in college but graduated later than she did, fiddled around in search of his ideal "alternative lifestyle" without ever settling down on any particular profession—the result being the twenty-million-won loan he had taken out and used up without her knowledge.

Saying he would pay it back, her husband promised he would do whatever it took. She knew he was being sincere. But she also knew that the world was not such an easy place as to hand over twenty million won to anyone based on their sincerity alone.

So she looked into whether her husband could use their mutual assets as collateral to take out any more money without her knowledge. She considered dropping his name from the deed somehow, but the taxes were simply too complicated. Still, it seemed like it was legally impossible for him to put up any shared property as collateral without her consent. But in the worst-case scenario, she would only be able to hold on to half of her property; this frightened her.

Their livelihoods depended on their home. And to her, home meant something far more than just a monthly source of income. The place was everything she had, the only thing to show for years of smashing herself against the world. And during that entire time she had worked herself to the bone, carrying her husband on her back, he had never so much as lifted a finger to help her. In the midst of her anxiety over the twenty million won of debt he had spent without her knowledge, all of these facts were beginning to seem very clear to her now.

When he felt like it, her husband would occasionally go hiking at a nearby foothill. He was never away long enough for her to worry about him, but there was no consistent pattern to his hikes. Sometimes he left early in the morning, sometimes he took days off from his habit before setting off abruptly in the evening. Ever since his friend had run away with his money, he would spend hours on the phone in the office before tiring of it and going for a walk in the hills.

She received the phone call when he was out on one of these hikes. She had gone down to the office to retrieve him for lunch, but there was only his cell phone at his desk. And just as she stepped in the office, it began to ring as if it had been waiting for her.

Was there finally someone who wanted some of the health drink? There was a spark of hope in her heart as she picked up the phone. At the sound of her voice saying, "Hello," whoever it was on the other end of the line went silent for a moment. The woman repeated her greeting and added, "Please speak up."

—Is it you, bitch?

The woman was taken aback by the hostility of the female voice on the other end. "Excuse me?"

—Are you that asshole's wife?

"What?"

The voice on the other end seethed with hate.

—Isn't it your bastard husband who tricked my husband into selling that bullshit berry drink, before your husband took our money and cut off my husband?

Finally, the call was starting to make sense. And who was accusing whom of being in the wrong! "Now look here. About that business, I—

—You made my husband put the business in his name so he would take all the blame, but you and your despicable man held onto the stock and grabbed the sales money for yourselves, am I right? My husband was the one who brought in all of his connections, but you two just sucked him dry and tossed him over when you were done with him!

"We were the ones who were ripped off! How dare you—"

But her raised voice was countered by an even louder attack reinforced by harsh curses. When the woman told her to watch her tone, the caller gave out a contemptuous laugh.

—Look at her standing by her man. Do you still want to stand by him when he's screwing some other woman? He hired some whore calling herself an interior designer when he was remodeling. Stealing other people's money, and having an affair right under your nose. What a pathetic household you run.

"What!"

The woman's agitated tone seemed to bring satisfaction to the caller, who began speaking in a more leisurely tone.

—I've got your husband's texts and calls as evidence, he's not going anywhere. Did you think I was going to pretend like nothing had happened?

The woman wanted to ask her what the evidence was for. But the caller seemed to have gone past the anger and cursing stage and entered the lamenting-her-fate stage.

—My husband is the real idiot for associating with such filth like you two, quitting his good job so he can go into business with his college buddies ... You two were probably fake students, right? Pretending to be college kids? A couple of grifters!

The moment the caller began to get all riled up again, she heard someone punching in the code to the main door downstairs.

Her husband. This surprised her so much that, for reasons she couldn't understand, she quickly hung up the phone.

She heard him come up the stairs. Swiftly, she put the phone back where it was and went to the fridge. She began rifling through its contents. It had been cleaned after her husband's friend had disappeared, but the fresher berries they had saved were starting to rot as well.

More keypad noises. It came from the second floor; it wasn't her husband but the tenants coming back from lunch.

She sighed in relief.

The phone lay mute on the desk.

The words "texts and calls" refused to leave her mind.

As did the passcode to her husband's phone.

She couldn't decide whether it was a good or bad thing that the blood-sausage place on the first floor chose that moment to raise the issue of the premium.

First, the old man came alone. Since it was the woman who mostly dealt with the renters, he had probably thought it would be easy for him, a man who had experienced the world, to get a young woman to do whatever he told her to. But the woman's husband, unusually for him, decided to lend his masculine presence to this meeting for reasons unknown.

When the old man mentioned the premium, the woman's husband countered with his understanding of the relevant legal facts. The old man reminded him that they had signed a modified contract to avoid transaction fees and threatened to report him to the tax offices. Undaunted, her husband continued to call the man "sir" and repeatedly explained the situation to him. "That contract was signed by both parties, and if you follow through with that threat, you will also be prosecuted by the tax offices. Also, your rent is actually not that high, nor have you paid it for a long time, which means whatever money we owe isn't going to be that high, either. Don't you think that it would be cheaper for us to just pay the back taxes than pay the thirty million won difference in a premium that has nothing to do with the landlord anyway? Don't you think so, sir?"

This set off the old man, who kept repeating "Young people don't know what's what these days" and "Let's see what happens when you stay on your high horse" before getting up and leaving. And it wasn't long after that when the old man came in with an "assistant" who was dressed entirely in black. A veiled threat that if the woman and her husband did not hand over the thirty million won, they would be inflicting a lot more than just monetary damage.

"We'll record them next time and have the lot arrested," said the woman's husband, unfazed as usual.

Whether there would be a "next time" to record and report was the question on the woman's mind. And the word "record" brought on a flood of memories of when she answered his phone and the things she discovered. This frustrated her so much that she could no longer speak, and her husband mistook her silence for acquiescence and was satisfied. That was the end of their conversation.

In the basement, as she played with the child, the woman suddenly burst into tears.

When the child asked her what was wrong, the first thing that came to the woman's mind was the face of the old man from the blood-sausage stew restaurant. They simply did not have thirty million won on hand to pay them off—nor were they even legally obliged to. But they couldn't afford the back taxes, either. Her husband had already spent the twenty million won he had borrowed, the third floor was still vacant, and the first floor, declaring their intent to move out soon, had been refusing to pay rent since the previous month.

"It's all right," said the woman as she shook her head and forced a smile. "Sometimes, adults get into complicated situations."

She tried to raise the corners of her mouth, but tears kept leaking from her eyes.

The child crouched before her and gazed wordlessly at the woman as she cried.

The blood-sausage restaurant owner never did get her premium.

The owner's husband was found dead in the kitchen of their restaurant. When his body was discovered, it was said that a part of his corpse had been boiling in the giant stockpot they used to make broth.

As the police descended on the crime scene to investigate

the grisly murder, the likes of which had never been heard of before in the neighborhood, the owner's daughter and son-in-law, who were said to have been employess there, suddenly vanished without a trace.

A few days later, the woman saw in the papers a photo of the black-clad "assistant" the old man had brought with him that time. According to the accompanying article, the assistant was a gangster who had been found dead in the bed of his lover.

This lover, who had discovered the body, stated to the police that she had left for work after seeing he was still asleep but had found him lifeless upon her return. The man's upper body had been crushed in a strange shape, leading the police to suspect that a rival gang had taken some kind of revenge on him.

Even as she played with the child in the basement, the woman couldn't shrug off these strange events.

But not being threatened was admittedly a good thing. There was no one to report them to the tax office or demand the difference on their premium, which meant she didn't have to worry about money for the time being. The clothing boutique that had been planning to move into the first floor was now dithering between breaking their signed lease or pushing back their move-in date, but the woman didn't have to worry about such things anymore.

Clunk

The woman looked up in surprise. The child had brought forth a new locked box from somewhere and was playing with it in front of her. This one had a simple lock that released when it was twisted. The child seemed amused by repeatedly locking it shut and then twisting the lock open. As the woman stared at the brightly smiling child's hands locking and twisting open the contraption, she was suddenly reminded of a line in the news article she had read earlier: "The body's torso had been crushed into a particular shape ..."

Clunk

The child looked up at the woman and smiled proudly.

Life is a series of problems. Especially when one is married and has a family. Because even when you manage to avoid the problems of the outside world and return home safely, your family is there waiting with a whole different set of problems of their own.

Although the issue with the blood-sausage stew place's premium was resolved (albeit in a way that left a queasy feeling in the woman's stomach), the caller did not relent with her attacks. They'd been receiving calls long before that, but her husband did not pick up on purpose and the woman didn't have any strength left over to make an issue of it. This agitated the caller even more. The caller somehow got the woman's private number and began to harass the woman on her own phone as well.

—Your husband is sleeping with the interior designer!

—You pretending to not see makes me sure that you're a scammer, too!

—The three of you went to college together, I'm convinced

you were the one who introduced the interior designer to your husband!

—I know you are the one who goaded your husband into having an affair and ripping off my husband and that you're only pretending to be a victim!

—Make your husband return the money he stole and tell me where my husband is!

—I can't breathe with these creditors coming after me. Tell me where my husband is or take legal responsibility for his debts!

The more the woman listened to the caller, the more she thought of this wife of her husband's friend as mentally ill or something close to it. She could almost pity her. Because, from the caller's perspective, her husband had simply said he was going into business before one day disappearing altogether, and now creditors were swarming around her, demanding to be paid.

But the woman herself could not afford to help this other woman who cursed and shouted down the phone at her at all times of the day.

According to the incendiary text messages saved on her husband's phone, he and the interior designer had been seeing each other for a long time. The twenty million won her husband had said he'd invested in his friend's defunct company had actually been handed over to this interior designer. Her husband's friend had never asked for the office to be remodeled. All he had said to him was, "If you have an empty office in your building, can I use it for just two months?" And when her husband had begun remodeling, his friend had messaged, in a disconcerted tone, "You're going to too much trouble for me, I just need a place to sit down for two months."

But her husband had wanted to show off to his lover that he was the owner of a building. "If you need more money for the construction, let me know and I'll get you whatever you need," he had boasted to her. The woman realized that it had never crossed her husband's mind that the money he would use to get whatever she needed was borrowed, nor the fact that the building he wanted to show off had been bought through years of his wife's back-breaking labor.

The child was good at playing by herself; this time, the woman did not cry as she watched her. The child kept locking and unlocking the box—*clunk, clunk, clunk*—as the woman watched in silence, lost in her own thoughts.

The child, still playing with the box, looked up at her and smiled. The woman tried to smile back, but found that she could not.

Saying he was going for a hike, her husband left the house late one evening.

A heavy rain began to fall.

He never returned from the mountain.

There was a traffic accident on the nearby highway. A car skidded on the road and crashed into a guardrail. The woman driver had been taken to the ER but was comatose. The man who had been sitting in the passenger seat had flown out the car on impact and was found on a slope. His neck broken, he had died instantly.

After the death of the husband, the child followed the woman around all day, even while the woman was on the phone with her mother.

—Are you sleeping well? And eating?

"I never miss a meal. And I'm sleeping well." The woman gestured to the child to be careful as the little one ran across the living room floor, giggling all the way.

—And how's the building, are you OK in there? Getting some rent money?

"Yes, a boutique moved into the first floor, and the publisher on the second floor still pays rent every month."

—Do you ever go outside? I hope you're not holed up in there all day.

The child leaped into the woman's embrace. The woman stroked the child's hair.

She had just begun to notice that the contours of the child seemed clearer.

"Well ..." Her voice briefly trailed off. "It's pretty comfortable in here."

—But you've got to get out and get some fresh air now and then. You're still young and childless, and it's not like widows need to hide away from the world anymore. Go travel, meet some people ...

The child reached for her phone to try and take it. The woman shook her head. "No, Mom is on the phone right now."

—What? I couldn't hear you just now.

She spoke into the phone. "It's nothing, Mom."

—Is there someone in the house with you?

"No, who else would be here?"

The woman's mother sighed.

—I can't bear the thought of you being alone in there all the time. And you refuse to let me come and take care of you for a while—

"Mom." The woman cut her off before she started her lamentations again. "I'm comfortable the way I am now. I just need more time, some rest, and I'll have my wits about me again. I'll take care of everything then."

—Your mother-in-law isn't bothering you, is she?

"No, Mom. It's nothing like that." She had to get her mother off the phone. "Look, I'm boiling some laundry right now and I need to get it off the fire. I'll call you soon."

—All right. Be careful. Don't do too many chores, and get out of the house every now and then.

"Bye."

She hung up the phone.

Turning to the child, she said, "Well, it's just you and me now."

The child stopped running around and faced her. She smiled.

"Would you like to go on a trip with your mom?" the woman asked. "You've never been outside this building, right? Do you want to go outside, just the two of us? Shall we go somewhere far, far away?"

The child looked at the woman's face with an intense expression. Wordlessly and slowly, she shook her head.

The woman already knew. The child had always been here in this building. And she would never be able to leave.

As long as she was with the child, she would never leave this building, either.

And that wouldn't be so bad, she thought.

"Come here."

The woman opened her arms wide. The child ran in for a hug. The woman almost fell backwards from the impact.

At first, the child had only been a faint shadow in the basement.

Now she had solid form, with real warmth and a soft texture to her skin. She was bigger, weightier, and clearer.

This made the woman feel immensely proud.

"You and Mom, the two of us are going to live together," she whispered to the pale shadow-child she held in her arms. "We're going to be happy here forever."

She kissed the child's soft, white forehead.

This trace of a small child, who had waited for her mom for so long in the black basement of a dark concrete building, looked up at the woman she had been searching for and gave a bright smile.

Ruler of the Winds and Sands

0

In the air above a sandy desert floated a ship made of golden gears. Sunlight glinted on each and every tooth of the thousands of gears that went *tick-tick-tick*, making the airborne vessel shine as brilliantly as the sun. This shimmering, flashing ship of gears slowly traversed the hot air above the desert sands, buoyed by the boiling heat and golden waves of reflected light that surrounded its hull.

1

The master of the ship was said to be a great warrior and a powerful sorcerer. According to ancient lore, the king of the desert had battled the master of the boat for control over the land that stretched even beyond the horizon to the golden sun. In the final battle, the king managed to sever the master's left arm. The master of the golden ship, with blood spraying from his severed arm, shouted and cursed the king of the desert.

"You have taken my virility, and so I shall take that of your descendants! You have scattered my blood on these lands, and for that, none who rule these sands will ever be safe from harm."

The king of the desert did not believe in curses. As he watched the master of the golden ship ride his horse of golden gears up into the air undulating in the sunlight, the king smiled victoriously. Drops of blood dotted the path where the master of the golden boat passed. They boiled like little flames before immediately drying out in the suffocating heat, a sight that made the king of the desert laugh with such malicious will and volume that he clearly hoped it would carry over to the decks of the ship.

2

Not long after, the king of the desert had a son. The prince was born blind. The king's rage pierced the sky. The queen, overcome with disappointment, lingered a little before dying.

Left without a mother, the prince was raised by the servants and handmaidens of the palace. The handmaidens took great care of him, but their hearts were always filled with fear. The king of the desert was rage itself, and the prince was a curse. The servants and handmaidens, in trying to avoid that rage and the curse, stooped their backs low and kept their heads down at all times. This was why, even as they fed or clothed or rocked the prince to sleep at night, there was no love in their hearts for him.

In order to survive, children come to their own understanding of their place in their world. It looks as if children are limited in what they are conscious of, but they comprehend very quickly the intention of adults and the trust given to them, better and more precisely than adults themselves do. The prince grew up surrounded by beauty and riches, among people who were polite and well-mannered but had no sincerity. As far as the prince knew, that was just what the world and its people were like.

3

The prince became a boy, and after a little while, a youth. He was blind and, as the only issue of the desert king, the crown prince. And so, the king of the desert, when his son came of age, dispatched emissaries across the endless stretches of sand to the people who lived on the grass plains to ask for a princess who would be queen of the desert.

The ruler of the grass plains knew the prince of the desert was blind, and he made this his reason for refusing at first. But when he was presented with the silks and jewels that the emissaries had brought with them, he soon changed his mind. This was how the princess of the grass plains came to follow the emissaries to the desert where she was to be wedded to the cursed prince.

4

The wedding was set for three months hence. All the servants and courtiers busied themselves with seemingly endless wedding preparations. The sleepy palace in the desert suddenly turned into a hive of activity.

The prince was very curious about the princess of the grass plains who was to become his bride. He wondered whether she knew he was blind and why she would come all this way to marry him if she did, or how she would react if she didn't … The prince was well aware of the ancient tradition of the groom not meeting the bride before the wedding, but he was determined to know what kind of person his bride-to-be was before it was too late.

Ever since he was little, the prince had been familiar with the various shortcuts and hidden passages in the palace. Since no one suspected a blind prince would know of such paths, the prince was able to explore the palace to his heart's content and go wherever he pleased. Even the darkest corner where light didn't reach was not a problem for him, and the prince was able to hide wherever he desired in the palace. This was how, on a night while everyone else was asleep, he was able to creep into the inner chamber where the princess was being kept.

She was asleep. Listening to the steady breathing of this unfamiliar woman, the prince stood in place for a while, absolutely still.

The princess opened her eyes. The prince could not see this, and continued to stand there without realizing.

"Who are you?" demanded the princess. "Why are you in my chambers at this hour?"

The prince gave a start. But he managed to calm himself down and slowly replied, "I am here to meet my bride."

5

As the prince carefully felt her face, the princess closed her eyes and remained still. The touch of this stranger's fingertips on her face made her feel shy and ticklish; it also felt good, somehow. The feeling of doing something forbidden disconcerted her and scared her a little, but it was also pleasurable and secretly thrilling. She could feel herself blushing a little more each time the prince's fingertips caressed her face.

By the time he took his hand away, the princess was completely and utterly in love. But she didn't know whether that love was for the prince or for her own excited emotions.

"You are beautiful," the prince whispered. "If only I could see ... If only I could see my beautiful bride's face, just once ..." Large tears sprang from the prince's eyes.

"Please don't cry." The princess tried to console him. "You can touch my face any time you so desire, just like now. I will stay by your side for the rest of our lives."

"But I am not the only one who will end up in misfortune," the prince said as he continued to shed tears. "The master of the golden ship cursed my whole family. As long as my father's blood rules the sands, no one will be safe, he said."

The princess was taken aback. "But why? Who would make such a fearful curse?"

"It's because he was defeated in a war and lost one of his arms," explained the prince. "He said my father had taken his virility, so all my father's descendants would also have their virility taken from them." The tears rolled down his cheeks. "If you marry me, our children, and their children, they will all have useless bodies like mine. And when the master of the golden boat invades our land again, this country—ruled by a king with no virility—will immediately fall."

And the prince lowered his head and cried copiously.

The princess embraced the prince and tried to console him. Her shoulder became drenched with the prince's tears.

He was gone from her chambers before the sun rose. Sitting alone in the darkness, the princess stared into the brightening gray of the eastern sky. As she watched the golden-gear ship slowly crossing the firmament above the sun rising on the horizon, the princess made a decision.

She was going to go to the master of the golden ship and break the curse for the prince who was to become her husband and for her children who were to be born and their children too.

6

It was not easy, sneaking out of the palace. The princess was a bride whose wedding was imminent, a future queen no less. She was surrounded by handmaidens at all times, and even when she was alone in her room, there was always a guard posted right outside her door. Thus, when the prince again visited her chamber in the middle of the night, she asked for his advice.

"Not only are you beautiful, you are brave," marveled the prince. "I know a way out of the palace. But once you are out and find your way to the golden ship, you will have to face him on your own. Are you up to it?"

The princess was firm. "I must try. I'm not going to challenge him to a duel, I'm simply a defenseless woman who is asking for a favor. He wouldn't harm me, would he?"

"We don't know that. He is a cruel man ..." The prince sighed. "If only I could see, then I could accompany you ..."

The princess smiled gently. "If you could see, we wouldn't need to go see the master of the golden ship in the first place. Please do not resent me if I am unsuccessful in my petition."

"I would never." The prince gently cupped her chin in his hands. "I am only grateful you are being so brave for me."

"One more thing," the princess said. "Even if I succeed, the king will be most displeased to learn that I escaped the palace before the wedding. If I'm discovered on my way back, I may be banished to my country of birth forever."

"Do not worry. Everything you are doing is for me, and I shall protect you. You are my bride, my wife."

Instead of an answer, the princess kissed the prince's lips.

7

The prince led the princess to the back gate of the palace. There, at the gap where the stone wall had cracked slightly, the two lovers passionately embraced and kissed.

"Wait for me," whispered the princess.

"Come back safely," answered the prince.

The princess bowed her head as she carefully slipped out the gap in the wall. Allowing herself one look backwards toward the palace, she then gazed up at the moonless, starless sky where the ship of golden gears glinted coldly in the air.

She began to walk toward the ship.

8

The sun was merciless in the day, and the princess, having grown up on the grassy plains, was not used to walking for so long on hot sand. She found that it quickly exhausted her, and there was no real respite sitting on the scorching sand, which made her journey to the golden boat a long one.

When she reached the spot right below the floating ship, she rested for a moment in the ship's shadow and caught her breath. The sunbaked sands were still hot, but thanks to the ship above her head, it was slightly cooler in the shadow. It was the first fragment of shade she had encountered since walking the long distance from the palace.

As she steeled herself, the princess pondered over how she would get on board. The ship swayed a little from side to side in the air. There was no anchor or ropes about it. She was afraid it would sail away from her at any time, disappearing beyond the horizon once more.

Just then, the golden gears made loud creaking sounds as they started to turn.

From between the gears, a golden ladder was lowered.

As she stared in bewilderment, the ladder reached low enough to touch the sand.

The princess stood up. She walked to the middle of the boat's shadow and began to climb up the ladder. Heated by the sun, the rungs were hot to the touch, almost enough to sear her palms. The princess gritted her teeth and continued to make her way up the ladder, rung by rung.

When she got to the top and stepped onto the deck of the golden boat, the princess heard a low but deep and mysterious voice that seemed to encircle her.

"And how has a princess of the grassy plains made her way to the Ship of Time and Winds?"

The princess looked up.

There, stood the master of the golden ship.

9

Contrary to the princess's expectations, the master looked like an ordinary man. He wore no golden armor, his face was not made of gears, and his body was not of sand. His skin was copper-colored, his hair seemed to have faded in the sun and wind, and only his eyes flamed a bright gold. As the prince had mentioned, the master of the golden ship had no left arm, and the empty, pale sleeve of his sun-faded shirt fluttered with every breeze.

"Why do you seek the Ship of Time and Winds?" the master asked again.

He looked ordinary, but his voice was not that of a man. Its reverberations were like the loud footsteps of a beast in a cave or an earthquake tearing through the grassy plains.

The princess began to speak. "The curse—" Just then, a wind started to blow. Its heat and dust prevented the princess from finishing what she was saying. She could not see in front of her.

"The curse, I am here to ask you to lift it!" she shouted with all her might, once she realized the wind would not abate. "Please lift the curse that you cast on the king of the desert!"

"What curse?"

Despite the dust storm, the voice of the master came through clear and true. Even the wind seemed to vibrate with it.

"Please restore the prince's sight! Please allow our children and their children to be born whole!"

The winds suddenly ceased.

"But why?" asked the master of the golden ship in a quiet voice. The princess felt the golden boards beneath her feet and the very sands of the desert below them tremble with those words, and she, too, trembled in fear.

"To curse someone out of spite for losing a war is cowardly!" she shouted as she gathered her courage again. "Please admit your defeat and lift the curse. The prince is to become my husband, and his children my children."

"I did not curse him," replied the master. "I do not lower myself to curse mere men."

"You lie!" The princess was taken aback, but she pressed on. "Why else would the prince be blind from birth?"

"The truth is different from what the princess has been told," said the master. "They were cursed because they started the war. The air from the horizon to the sun and moon is a place man may not rule. My ship has sailed peacefully in that air since the dawn of time. It was the king of the desert, blinded by his greed for gold, who first drew his weapons." The voice of the master of the golden ship was calm. "Those who stare for too long at the sun are bound to go blind. The king of the desert made the foolish choice to brandish his sword at the sun. And his progeny will pay for his sins."

"Please lift the curse!" shouted the princess. "Or at least, tell me how to lift it! The prince of the desert has suffered since birth because of his father's wrongdoing. For the sake of his unborn children, the future king will never start a war. I give you my word. Please lift the curse!"

The master of the golden ship sighed. Again, the princess felt the golden planks beneath her feet tremble.

"All right," he said, slowly. "When the rains fall on the desert, release a blind fish into the sea. Then the curse shall be lifted from the prince." Before the princess could ask him what he meant, the master added a word of warning. "The true nature of man is different from what the princess understands. Even when the curse is lifted, the princess shall not wed the prince."

And the master of the golden ship lifted his only hand and made a light, flicking gesture.

The next moment, the princess was in the air. As softly as a feather, she swayed in the air before lightly landing on her feet.

10

The princess wandered the desert for a long time.

The place where the golden ship had put her down was not where she had first climbed the ladder. As she had been born and raised on the grassy plains, she had learned from an early age how to read the sun, moon, and stars to discern her position, which was how she could tell with some assurance where she was. But she was surrounded by sand as far as the eye could see, and the dunes shifted whenever the winds blew. No matter how the winds had blown on the grassy plains of her homeland, the land had never shifted shape nor had the trees and grass ever changed their positions. It was unfamiliar terrain to her, and she had no way of predicting how long it would take, walking across the dunes. All she could do was determine where southwest was by the sun and walk in that direction toward the palace.

What he had meant by the blind fish and how she was to find a sea in the middle of the desert—these were mysteries she could not fathom. And as she exhausted herself walking, the princess began to forget about any talk of fish.

She had brought with her some water and dried fruit when she set out from the palace, but that had been long finished by the time she reached the golden ship. The sandy dunes continued to change their shapes, endlessly appearing and reappearing before her. The princess was certain she would meet her death in the desert before she reached the palace.

11

The desert nights were cold. The same winds from the day blew during the night. If she tried to rest, sitting for a moment on the sands, the dune next to her would slowly but threateningly move toward her. If she did not want to get buried, she would have to get up and keep walking.

All feeling left her body as her legs mechanically propelled her forward. Each time she made a step, her foot sank into the sand.

She missed the grassy plains. She missed the flat and wide horizon uninterrupted by high sand dunes. She missed the hard and arid land, the grasses and tumbleweeds that thrived on it. Riding horses over that hard and wide earth, the hoofs striking against the firmness ...

The princess tripped over something firm and hard.

She sank into the sand. Quickly, she managed to raise herself out of danger, and she shook herself off and spat the sand out of her mouth before turning around to see what it was that had tripped her.

It was a large, bulky object protruding from beneath the sand.

In the time she had walked to the golden ship and then from it after disembarking, the princess had never felt anything hard about her feet. She crouched before the object and began to dig it out.

The night deepened. The princess, not even knowing what she was excavating, moved her hands without feeling anything. Other than thirst, hunger, and the cold. The thirst ... More than anything else, she was thirsty. Her arid homeland also had precious little water, but because she had been a princess, she never had to know how terrible thirst could be. The princess was thirsty enough to want to drink the sand she was shoveling away with her bare hands. Drink the sand ...

Just before she was about to drink in the sand she had scooped up in her palms, she quickly came to her senses.

12

The princess wept. Her throat was so dry that it felt like it was splitting into pieces and there was not a drop of liquid in her body, but amazingly there were still tears coming out of her eyes. Leaning against the huge thing she had been digging out, the princess let her tears flow. She was scared, cold, and unbelievably thirsty. *I'm going to die in the desert*, she thought. She would never see the morning again. Or the sunrise. Never again would she behold the blind prince desperately waiting for her in the palace, the grassy plains she had been born and raised on, her parents. She would die, sink into the sand, and her body would never be found. The thought made her cry even harder. Her tears became wails, and the princess threw herself upon the mysterious object in the middle of the desert, screaming her grief out into the desert night underneath the stars.

The bulky thing she had been leaning her forehead on was soon drenched in her tears.

She continued to cry.

The object her forehead was leaning against moved.

She threw herself back in surprise. Her tears stopped.

A giant fish was flailing in the sands.

The princess was so shocked, she started stumbling backwards before falling on her behind.

The thing protruding from the sand was the head of a fish. Even in the dim light of the moon, she could clearly make out the milky film clouding over a single eye.

"When the rains fall on the desert, release a blind fish into the sea."

The princess came to her senses. She immediately began to dig out the flailing fish from the sands.

Just a moment ago she had been exhausted and crying, but a strength she had not known she possessed now flowed through her. She furiously attacked the sand, first exposing the gills, then the backfin, and soon the body. After she had excavated the tail, the princess cautiously touched the fish's eye. With the gentlest brush of her fingertips, the thin, hard film over the eye shattered into flakes.

The fish swung its tail widely. It launched itself from the sands into the cold night sky. The moment it leaped for the sprinkling of stars against deep indigo, the princess heard a sound as if the night sky, clear as glass, was shattering.

Rain began to fall.

Water poured from the cracks in the sky. The princess got to her feet as cold, fresh water drenched her whole body. She opened her mouth to the rain and drank it all in. Even when her thirst was quenched many times over, she spread her arms to the sky and kept drinking in the rain, dancing with joy.

The blind fish had returned to the vast sea, and rain fell from the desert sky.

The princess was elated. Her fear of death, her homesickness, it was all forgotten. Who she was, why she was in the middle of the desert—she was so overjoyed that she forgot it all.

And the princess woke from her sleep.

Far away, she saw the gates of the palace.

13

The palace was bustling by the time the princess had returned. There was a festival going on in the courtyard, and soldiers gathered before the gate.

"The curse has been lifted! The prince can see!" shouted the soldiers as they ate and drank to their hearts' content. "God has willed for the curse to be lifted; this is a sign that we should kill the sorcerer!"

This alarmed the princess. As she jostled through the feasting soldiers and made her way toward the main palace building, she saw that the king was giving a speech from one of the balconies.

"... and when the sorcerer is slain, the golden ship will be ours! All the gold and jewels in the ship will belong to us, and with this flying vessel, we shall conquer even greater lands beyond the horizon!"

The prince, who was standing next to the king, opened his now-seeing eyes wide and shouted, "The gold is ours! All the world is ours!"

The soldiers, aristocrats, and servants roared in unison. It was enough to make the walls of the palace shake.

Fear gripped the princess.

"Was the master of the golden ship telling the truth?" she shouted up at the prince high above her. "That the war wasn't because of the land beyond the horizon but started because you were blinded by greed for gold?"

Silence fell upon the palace. All the people gathered beneath the balcony turned and stared at the princess.

The prince was the first to speak.

"Seize her!" he shouted, pointing to her. "She's a whore of the sorcerer! Seize her!"

At his command, the soldiers threw their wine goblets aside and dashed toward the princess.

She tried to run. But she was soon surrounded by the king's men. Before she had taken even two paces, she was caught.

"A witch! A traitor! A whore of the sorcerer, slandering the king to bring him down!" shouted the prince as he stared down at the princess struggling against the soldiers. "Kill her!"

At the prince's command, more soldiers appeared with their swords and spears.

The princess, held back by the soldiers, looked up at the prince on the balcony. The moment their eyes met, she became speechless. There was no recourse for objection or mercy in his gaze.

He was expressionless. The light that had found its way into his eyes was cold and lifeless. This strange man staring down at her and cruelly ordering her death was not the same prince who had shed tears on her shoulder.

The soldiers' swords came for her throat. Petrified, the princess shut her eyes tight.

In that moment, the wind began to blow.

14

Sandstorms swept the palace. No one could open their eyes or even breathe because of the flying dust, sand, and earth. The sand dug into the people's noses, ears, and mouths.

Without realizing it, the soldiers surrounding the princess dropped their weapons. Everyone frantically attempted to shield their faces, screwing their eyes shut and coughing.

And then came a rumbling noise. Screams ensued. The princess, through a crack in the fingers she had put over her face, watched as the balcony of the palace collapsed. The king and prince who had stood there fell with it, surrounded by the storm. Rocks and rubble fell over them.

The ground began to shake. The princess looked down. She could see the sand that covered the horizon sinking into ever-widening cracks.

When the ground beneath her feet gave way, the princess found herself floating in the air before she could scream. A familiar ticking noise surrounded her. Above her head was that shadow once more, the same shade that had once given her shelter.

Floating above the crumbling palace, the princess stared as the ship of golden gears leisurely crossed the desert sky.

15

The palace was completely destroyed. Not a single hewn stone in a wall remained where it had been. Once more on the decks of the golden ship, the princess gazed into the haze of dust that had once been the palace.

"This is not the fault of the princess," a low voice proclaimed, making the planks beneath her feet quake again. "One can break the curse, but it is impossible to cure their blindness from greed. They were always ready to wage another war."

The princess nodded, shaken. Like the dust cloud below, her thoughts were so foggy that she found it hard to think straight in that moment.

Something cold and moist touched her hand. Startled, the princess turned around.

The master of the golden boat was handing her a goblet of water. The goblet was smaller than the princess's hand. Despite the hot desert winds that raged around them, the water was as cold as ice, attracting water droplets to the surface of the goblet.

The princess slowly raised the goblet. Her lips touched its rim. Cold water flowed into her.

The goblet may have been smaller than her hand, but it poured forth an endless stream of water. She drank her fill. It seemed like an eternity since she had drunk such cool water. Perhaps it was the first time in her life.

"Stay here," said the soft voice that rang through the golden decks. "Rule the winds and sands with me, sail above the horizon of time. Until the day the sun and moon shatter and disappear, everything the stars and clouds can reach in this endless realm, it shall all belong to you."

The princess looked down at the goblet in her hand. She had drunk her fill, but it was full again in the blink of an eye. Water droplets gathered on the goblet again, and the cold moistness in her hand gave her a strangely lovely feeling.

"I wish to live as a mortal," she finally answered. "I wish to meet a man who is like me, who will cherish and love me as I do him, to have children, to see them grow up and find their own mates and have their own children ... That is the life I wish for."

"There is death at the end of such life." The master of the wind and sand's voice was soft.

The princess nodded. "I know. But I will live life fully until my very moment of death."

The man of the golden ship said, "I cannot give the princess the life of mortals, but I can still promise you a peace and eternity that they do not know."

The princess smiled. She nodded.

The man's empty left sleeve began to move. The princess felt a cool and soft breeze brush against her right cheek.

The gears of the golden ship began to creak and turn. As the ship changed course, the teeth of its gears shattered the sunlight into shimmering sparks. With the sun behind it, the golden ship began to slowly cross the desert sky toward the princess's home, the land of the grassy plains.

Reunion

This love story is for you.

No one asked us, when we weren't famous
Whether we wanted to live or not
I expected so many things
But didn't know what I wanted ...

I was sitting on the southern side of the plaza. Nursing a mug of cheap mulled wine, the kind they sell everywhere on the streets in the winter. Mulled wine is a European winter drink made of red wine that's simmered for a long time with spices like cinnamon and cloves. The alcohol evaporates somewhat in the heat, but it's not entirely boiled away so there's just enough left over to get drunk on. Which was why sipping this hot beverage in freezing cold weather was making my head spin a little.

"Czy kogoś szukasz?" *Are you looking for someone?*

I turned my head. He smiled at me.

He opened his arms. I stood up. We embraced. He further

greeted me with a kiss on each cheek. Awkwardly, I reciprocated. No matter how glad I was to see someone, greeting with kisses still felt strange to me.

"Mogę?" *May I?* He indicated the seat next to me.

I smiled and nodded.

"Wiedziałem, że będziesz," he said. "Czekałem na Ciebie."

I knew you would come. I've been waiting for you.

*

A long time ago, I met him in the plaza for the first time. Poland's summers are hot and dry—I was holding a cold drink in one hand and sitting in the shade. My life was making me anxious. I wanted to escape from it, for just a little while at least.

The plaza was full of people but the voices that drifted toward me were mostly speaking English or German rather than Polish. The city was a tourist town. Nine out of ten people sitting under the statue in the center of the city plaza were from abroad. I was one of these foreigners, and like other foreigners, I was sitting by the plaza's statue at an outdoor café, staring at the sunlight heating up the paving stones.

Then I saw the old man.

I didn't spot anything different about him at first. Again, there were many people in the plaza, and the countless foreigners were taking pictures, drinking beer, talking on phones, talking to each other. Living in the moment, so to speak. There were people moving slowly, people just standing around, and people moving about in a hurry. There were people with dogs and people with children. It wouldn't have been easy spotting someone doing something strange in that crowd.

But the main reason I was paying attention to the old man was because for one thing, he was walking with a very pronounced limp. Another reason was that despite his limp, he moved with surprising agility.

The third reason I kept watching the old man was because he was only walking on one side. I need to explain this a little more.

The plaza was roughly the shape of a square, with a statue of a nineteenth-century Romantic poet who was considered a treasure of the nation placed in the middle. The reason it was "roughly" a square shape was because while the plaza had roads on all sides, there were also little alleys radiating from the center. A typical European city plaza, with the northern side—the side the poet's statue faced—lined with souvenir shops, and to the west, a little away from the poet statue, a clock tower, and to the east and south of the plaza, outdoor cafés, pubs, and restaurants. I was sitting with my back to the poet statue, looking south.

The old man appeared on my left and walked toward my right. Limping at a surprisingly rapid speed, he crossed the main road and disappeared into an alley. Then just five minutes later, he reappeared to my left at exactly where he had first come from and walked to the right. Swiftly limping all the way, he moved in a straight line to cross the main street on the right and disappeared once more into an alley. And again, he reappeared to my left not five minutes after. With his mouth firmly shut, slightly biting down on his bottom lip, and his eyes opened wide, his face frozen into a desperate expression, he diligently moved his uncomfortable leg to walk, right before my eyes, from the plaza's east to west in a straight line.

The plaza was wide. It took about fifteen to twenty minutes for the old man to traverse the southern side of the plaza on his bad leg with his wobbling walk. Even if he had taken a shortcut that I didn't know about, it should've taken him at least twenty minutes to circle back to the square if it had taken him twenty minutes to get to the alley. But the old man would disappear and reappear barely five minutes later in the exact same spot. And limp the same distance at a fearsome speed. In a single direction, over and over again.

"Czy Ty też go widzisz?" *You can see him, too?*

Startled, I turned my head. The man, who stood with the sun to his back, looked like a giant from where I sat.

"Mogę?" *May I?*

The man was pointing at the chair next to me. I just nodded. In all honesty, I was already taken aback by the old man, and now this giant, wherever he came from, was also so unnerving that I couldn't find my voice.

The man came and sat down next to me.

For the next hour, the man and I said nothing to each other as we watched the old man. And the old man, seemingly unexhausted, kept walking and walking in the same direction as before with his limp.

Sitting there with the tall man, I discovered something else about the old man we were observing. It was the height of summer but the old man wore long black slacks and a khaki-colored sweater, and despite the sun beating down on him, he didn't seem at all tired or hot. I couldn't see if he was sweating from where I sat, but at least he didn't make any motions to wipe his sweat away. And no matter how closely I watched him, I had no idea where he was trying to go or how he managed to return to his original spot so quickly.

"Przypomina mi o dziadku," the man next to me murmured.

I looked at him.

"He reminds me of my grandfather," he said again in English.

Most Polish people don't expect foreigners to understand Polish. Since I had no understanding of the situation—who he was, why he was talking to me, or who the old man was—I decided not to get into it. I said nothing.

The man didn't seem to mind either way.

"He was lost, my grandfather," he said. "Just like him."

Naturally, my eyes returned toward the old man he was pointing at.

The old man was no longer there. This was unsettling. I stood up and looked around for him, but he was nowhere to be seen.

"On wróci," the man mumbled. "Zawsze wraca."

He'll be back. He always returns.

The man stood up, nodded at me, and left.

*

It was in a library where I met the man again.

I was finishing up my graduate studies back then and was in Poland on a research trip. My university had given me some funding, but that money barely covered the cost of the plane ticket. Housing, bus fare, even the price of getting copies made at the library, all that I had to pay out of pocket. And there was no guarantee that I would come out of all this with anything to show for it. But I wanted to finish what I had started, and the most immediate and tangible way I could accomplish that was to borrow books from the library.

Like many libraries in Eastern Europe, the university library I had made my pilgrimage to had closed stacks. I had to find the call number for each book, fill out a slip for each one, and a librarian would go into the stacks to fetch the book for me. So I wrote my slips and handed them over to the librarian at the circulation desk, who happened to be that man.

Neither he nor I spoke a word of greeting or recognition. He matter-of-factly picked up the slips, flipped through them for a moment, and told me to come back two hours later. I nodded and decided to go back to my seat and look for more material.

Two hours later when I returned to the desk, the man presented a stack of books to me and said, "Więc mówisz po polsku?" *So you speak Polish?*

"Tak." *Yes.*

A question I had been asked on numerous occasions. I answered simply. The man looked at my stack and asked me another question.

"Druga wojna światowa?" *The Second World War?*

I couldn't answer him. I had just picked up the books and was trying to keep my balance, pressing down on the top of the stack with my chin. The man stopped asking me questions. And so, hugging the books, I gingerly turned around and went back to my seat.

It was because I could see the old man, and also because I was researching the Second World War, he told me later. I had a feeling that was the case. There was probably some racial curiosity involved as well but I didn't ask about that. All I did was read in the library during the day and come out to the plaza in the evenings for a simple dinner and some people-watching. Prices in Poland at the time were very low, and I could afford a meal even in that touristy section of town, as long as I stuck to the outdoor cafés and didn't go into the restaurants. I would grab a bottle of sparkling water and a sandwich, watch the people coming and going and the carriage for tourists going round and round the plaza, and try not to think of the future. I didn't believe in any bright future for me. I didn't know if I would even be able to make a living. Therefore, "a moment ago" was always the best moment, and the present was always better than the future. When I returned, I knew I would miss leisurely sitting in this spot, enjoying the slowly setting sun. I tried my utmost to enjoy it as much as I could.

I had finished my day at the library and was in the plaza, looking around for an empty table at an outdoor café, when the man appeared.

"Piwo?" *Beer?*

A short question. After a moment of brief hesitation, I nodded.

*

From then on, whenever I left the library and went to the plaza, he would appear before me after a little while. Or, on the days I wasn't working at the library, he would wait for me there. During our simple dinners he would mostly drink beer, and I would drink coffee or sparkling water.

I never saw the old man again.

"On kiedyś tu wróci," he said. *He'll come back here someday.*

I laughed. "That's the title of a Polish language textbook one of the universities here publishes."

"I know," he answered, smiling.

The title was actually *Pewnego dnia tu wrócisz ponownie —You'll Come Back Here Someday*. I didn't believe I'd ever be back. As much as I loved the place, life doesn't give such opportunities so readily, and I couldn't continue this state of hovering between reality and unreality forever.

That was probably why, when he suggested we go to his apartment, I accepted.

... If I could make a wish
I wouldn't know what to say
What should I wish for
Bad times or good times ...

*

He asked me to tie him up. The tools, methods, and positions differed slightly each time, but he was always very thorough in explaining what he wanted.

He was asking me to tie him up, not the other way around, and it seemed like such an important thing to him that I didn't ask any questions and just did it. It goes without saying that I had never tied up a person before in my life. Even tying knots was awkward for me. Patiently, he explained what he wanted over and over again and was grateful when I had bound him up tightly in the way he wanted.

It wasn't so much a fetish as it was an obsession. He had a fixed script for the whole thing from beginning to end. Only when he and the other person (me, in other words) followed this script precisely could he calm down. But if one thing went off-script, he became very anxious and repeatedly asked me to correct it until we followed the script precisely once more. But that script was solely his own, and the problem was that I didn't know it at first.

On the surface, I was the one doing the tying and he the one being tied, but in practice, he was the one ordering me around and I the one trying to adhere to the script. He didn't seem aware that he was following some imaginary script. He kept using words like "correct" or "wrong" to describe my attempts. But on a fundamental level, there is no wrong or right way of tying up your lover in bed. It was tough for me when I didn't understand his highly subjective judgment regarding what was correct or wrong. He would patiently repeat himself or try using easier words, but that only made me feel like I was stupid. He wasn't angry when I was "wrong," but I could see he was getting nervous, which made me feel even more stupid and useless.

"I'm sorry." He would apologize when I seemed frustrated. "I know this is unpleasant. I know I'm strange, too. But please, bear with me."

I didn't think tying him up was in itself unpleasant or strange. There are many kinds of tastes in the world, and if I had found his so unacceptable, I wouldn't have stayed. I just wanted to do something that was important for him because I didn't dislike him as a person, and to do that, I had to understand the general picture he possessed in his head, the script he stored in his mind.

It took quite some time for me to understand the context. His apartment, to speak in Korean terms, was a "one-room." Small and narrow, but the ceiling very high, with a skylight through which you could see the stars. Gazing at my body and his own tied-up self reflected on the glass panes above us against the black night, he would murmur, "Beautiful."

I'd nod mechanically. From my perspective, things were a little too unreal for me to really appreciate them. Things like Poland, this tied up man, myself.

Then, he told me about his grandfather.

*

It was the summer of his eleventh year when he went to live with his grandfather. His grandfather had survived the Nazi concentration camps. Not only did the Nazis have the notorious death camps with their gas chambers, they also ran munitions factories using forced labor. This was where many Polish people with no Jewish ancestry ended up. When labor was in short supply toward the end of the war, the Germans would roam the streets snatching up anyone they could find to send to munitions factories or farms. His grandfather was one of the people who had been taken from the streets.

"But Grandfather never told me what life had been like in the camp. Not even once. Isn't that strange?"

It genuinely seemed to perplex him.

His Grandfather was taken up with other concerns. According to his grandson, the older man's purpose in life could be summed up in one word: "survival."

The old man never left the house. His life consisted of practicing how to survive without ever leaving his home. Once the sun went down, it was forbidden to turn the lights on or even turn the faucets to take a shower, as was making any kind of sound. They spared their water and food as much as possible, which was why their home was always stacked with canned food.

"My favorite times were Easter and Christmas and Catholic saints' days. We got to eat things that weren't from a can."

His grandfather also regularly cleaned the house and did the laundry—their home was as neat as a pin and their clothes were immaculate. But there were always fully packed suitcases by the door in case they ever needed to make a run for it. A crucial part of his life with his grandfather was checking the contents of those bags, making sure the food and batteries were regularly replaced.

He tried to understand his grandfather and followed the

rules to the best of his ability. But the year he turned fifteen, he rebelled against his grandfather for the first time. His grandfather had stopped him from going out with his friends after the winter sun had set. The reason was not to simply make his grandson obey him, but because he was so afraid and anxious. It was precisely because his grandson understood this that made him snap at his grandfather.

"I shouted at him that the war was long over, Communism was dead, everyone was free, and nothing bad happened to children who played outside past seven p.m."

"What did he say to that?"

"He said nothing."

His grandfather had stared at him for a while, turned around, and went into his room. His unfocused eyes and slumped shoulders made him look as if he'd aged ten years in a single moment.

From then on, his grandfather stopped buying canned food or keeping bags by the front door. Until the day he graduated high school, all his grandfather did was sit gazing blankly into a television screen. He died in front of that television.

"He was dead when I came home one day. And right next to him stood a younger version of him. About the age I am now, the way he looked before he was taken to the concentration camp."

His grandfather's younger self kept agitatedly looking back and forth between his older self's face and his grandson's. The grandson slowly pointed to the door. When he nodded, his grandfather's younger self, still with a confused expression, slowly walked toward it and departed. From a window, the grandson stared for a long time as his grandfather's soul walked down the street, crossed the sunlit plaza, and disappeared into a wider realm.

"Grandfather had spent his whole life being terrified of a war that was long over, of a concentration camp that had long disappeared. It was only after he died when he could finally walk about the city freely," he murmured.

I had to ask him. "Who was that older gentleman walking in one direction in the plaza?"

"Probably someone shot during the war," he said. "I've seen him there often. He crosses the street and tries as hard as he can to go back home, but I think he lost so much blood that he died before he could make it."

"I wonder why they can't leave those terrible times behind. Whether in life or death."

"Trauma. Probably."

... If I could make a wish
I want to be just a little happier
If I become too happy
I will miss sadness

He occasionally hummed a song under his breath. I asked him what it was once, and he said he didn't know. "Some song my grandfather sang often. Probably from the war."

A long time later, I heard the song again in an old movie. It was about World War II and the Nazi concentration camps, and the main female protagonist slightly altered the lyrics of a Marlene Dietrich song.

Life
I love life
... I don't know what I want but
I still expect a lot

In the movie, a woman imprisoned in a concentration camp seduces a Nazi officer in order to survive, serenading him half-naked. A life destroyed, not knowing what one wants, but loving life nevertheless—the lyrics resurrected my long-forgotten friend, and thoughts of him lingered for a long time.

*

The summer was short, and I had to go back. When I had only a few days left, I asked him a question.

"What is the sadness you miss that makes you want to be tied up?"

There was conflict in his gaze. It was a long time before he spoke.

"No one has asked me that before."

"Are you happy when you're tied up?" I asked.

"No," he immediately replied. And then, after some thought, he added, "It feels safer when I'm tied up."

"What feels safer?"

He always wanted me to tie him up as tightly as I could. It was clear he was in pain when I did, and there were red welts where the restraints had been when I untied him. Even if I was physically weaker than him, and even if I was his lover, I found it hard to believe that such tight knots made him feel safe.

Slowly, he whispered, "I feel like I'm being given permission to stay alive."

His reply was somehow so heart-breaking that I tied him up with all my might.

*

When I met him again, he was still in the same apartment. It had been a long time and I couldn't remember clearly, but his apartment seemed emptier and more desolate than before.

"I thought you'd be married by now," I said.

"I almost was."

"Why didn't you do it?"

"She didn't want to tie me up."

I nodded.

"And you?" he asked. "Why aren't you married?"

For a moment, I thought about the simplest way to answer this question. "I have debts to pay," I said finally. "Mother borrowed some money under my name."

And was still borrowing it. I didn't know how to say "forgery of official documents" in Polish so I couldn't go into more detail.

He nodded as if he understood and left it at that. I liked that about him.

"Is that gentleman in the plaza still there?" I asked.

"Probably. He's only visible in the summer usually, I haven't seen him lately."

That old man repeatedly walking from east to west on the southern side of the plaza was the only ghost I ever saw. Whether before the plaza or after, in Korea or another country, I had never seen another ghost. Until now.

"Really?" He was surprised. "You were so casual about it that I thought you saw ghosts all the time."

Since he was four, he had seen things other people didn't. Dead people, but also dead animals like cats, dogs, or horses. Too young to understand what death was, the sight of half-transparent people and animals floating through surrounding objects was simply amusing to him.

Like most Polish people, his parents were Catholics. When he began describing what the dead animals looked like, his mother thought he simply had an overactive imagination; it was only when he could accurately describe what people had looked like right before their deaths that she became terrified. She prayed and consulted with a priest and spent most of the day in church with him, but it was no use. Even in the church, he could see a priest who had died there two years ago and the man whose funeral they had held the other week. His mother brought him back and starved him, and when he complained about being hungry, she beat him.

The beatings had an instant effect, and he no longer talked about the dead people or animals he saw. But making him fast had backfired, as hunger sharpened his sensitivity. Especially when he went to bed on an empty stomach, he would talk to the dead in his sleep or sleepwalk with dead people in the middle of the night. This horrified his mother, who would forbid him from eating all day and lock him in the house, beating him mercilessly. His mother always cried as she hit him and prayed fervently afterward. He knew that his mother stayed home all day with him also eating nothing and not sleeping and crying all night, praying in whispers, and that was why the more he was beaten, the guiltier he felt. In his eleventh year, his mother's maternal uncle—in other words his grandmother's brother—passed away. When his mother came back from the funeral, he said goodbye to his mother in the voice of his grandmother's brother whom he had never met. He had no memory of this himself. His mother did not eat for days after that and was hospitalized, which was why he was sent to his grandfather's house in this city. This was when I learned for the first time that he was not from this southern city but from the outskirts of Warsaw.

"Then is your mother still in Warsaw?"

"Probably," he replied. "I never saw her after being sent away to my grandfather's. Except briefly at my high school graduation. We haven't been in contact since."

"And your father?" He had never spoken about his father. His expression was so disconcerted that I apologized. "I'm sorry."

"No, it's not that. My father is ... how do I say this ..." He frowned. "My father was ... an uncertain person. Do you know what I mean?"

I did not. I waited.

"When I was with Mother or Grandfather, the purpose of my existence was clear. Does that make sense? Grandfather's purpose was to survive using the means he learned in the war, and therefore he always had something to do. Check the emergency bags, check the water and cans, at night turn the lights off and don't make a sound. When the sun rose the next day, he had a clear sense of having survived to see another day. With Mother ..." He trailed off and was lost in thought. "With Mother things were bad, but my purpose then was that she was suffering because I was bad, so I had to not be bad. When I said bad things she would cry, she would starve and pray, tie me up on the bed and hit me, and sometimes leave me tied up all night so I wouldn't go off on a walk with a dead person. So not being bad was my purpose. But my father ..." He frowned again. "Well, Father is my grandfather's son. But he was totally different from Grandfather. I don't know what he lived for. He didn't seem happy or anything. He was always doing something meaningless while his mind was elsewhere." He thought a bit more. "I don't know about Father. I'm not in contact with him."

I could finally understand the horrific and cruel clarity of what he considered to be meaningful. The desperation and immense fear that your life, as well as the future to come, hinged on a moment. I could also understand how, in a situation where there was a single person who could kill you but also save you, all your survival instincts would be used toward satisfying that one person.

Once you experience a terrible trauma and understand the world from an extreme perspective, it is difficult to overcome this perspective. Because your very survival depends on it.

Parents who destroy their children's lives, who suck the life out of their children's futures, not only for the sake of maintaining their own illusions but also to zealously expand them into the lives of their children—such parents can almost be understood from the perspective of obsession. Following the words "Be grateful I raised you" is the implied clause "instead of killing you or leaving you for dead." They probably mean it, too. My parents and their parents' generations, after surviving the Korean War, had always, just like the generation that survived World War II, set their purpose not to live a human life but to have an animal's instinct for survival.

Still, understanding and forgiving are completely different things.

He whispered, "Will you tie me?"

I nodded.

"Will you be able to leave after the night is over?" I asked.

"I don't know." Then he said, "What are you going to do after I'm gone?"

I couldn't answer. He asked again. "Will you go back to your country?"

"No," I said. "I will never go back again." My own answer surprised me.

Quietly, he said, "Then I will stay here with you."

"Thank you," I whispered back.

When I woke up the next morning, he wasn't with me. I opened the bathroom door. Just as he had looked when he died, he was hanging by the neck from a radiator, his eyes closed.

I tapped him lightly. He opened his eyes.

"Do you want me to untie you?"

His throat was constrained by the cord around it, so he blinked in answer.

As I undid the cord, I listlessly sang along with him.

... If I could make a wish
I wouldn't know what to say.
What should I wish for
The bad times or the good times

I had no hope anymore for good times, but I didn't want to wish for bad times, either. I was waiting for something but didn't know what to hope for. There was no future. All of our survival skills were trapped in the past.

For some people, their lives are ruled by one shocking event reverberating through their survival instincts. Life shrinks into a trap made up of a shimmering moment in the past, a trap where they endlessly repeat that singular moment when they were surest of being alive. That moment is short, but long after it has passed, good times as well as bad slip like sand through their fingers as they meaninglessly repeat and confirm their survival. Those who are unaware of their lives slipping away while they are ensnared in the past—him, his grandfather, his mother, me—are in the end, whether alive or dead, ghosts of the past.

... If I could make one wish
I want to be just a little bit happier
If I'm too happy
I will miss the sadness

I released his neck and wrists.

"How did you do this?" I marveled. "How did you tie your own hands and noose?"

"I thought about it for a long time." He seemed slightly proud of himself. "I had to do it alone, because if I made a mistake, I wouldn't die but only get hurt, and that would mean a lot of suffering."

I hugged him hard. I imagined him alone in that empty apartment, pondering for a long time the most efficient way of hanging himself.

"It's all right," he said. "Thank you."

And he was gone. I was alone in his empty bathroom.

No one asked us, when we were still nameless
Whether we wanted to live or not
Now I wander the big city alone
Looking in doors and windows
Waiting and waiting for something ...

There was nothing left for me to wait for.

But there I remained, standing in his bathroom, waiting for someone to miraculously find me, to release me from my ties to this life.